Was Val real Guy?

He was a wonderful man, kind, clever, funny, passionate and a superb doctor. . .everything she could ever need.

But in the back of her mind there was a terrible suspicion—had her subconscious had a hand in the growing attraction? Had she recognised that under the cover of his beard was the man who could be mistaken for her husband's twin?

Josie Metcalfe lives in Cornwall now with her long-suffering husband, four children and two horses, but, as an Army brat frequently on the move, books became the only friends who came with her wherever she went. Now that she writes them herself she is making new friends, and hates saying goodbye at the end of a book—but there are always more characters in her head clamouring for attention until she can't wait to tell their stories.

Recent titles by the same author:

A WISH FOR CHRISTMAS
FOR NOW, FOR ALWAYS
WORTH WAITING FOR
LOUD AND CLEAR
FORGOTTEN PAIN
BOUND BY HONOUR
A VOICE IN THE DARK

VALENTINE'S HUSBAND

BY
JOSIE METCALFE

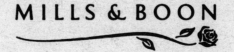

MILLS & BOON

*First published in Great Britain 1997
Harlequin Mills & Boon Limited,
Eton House, 18-24 Paradise Road, Richmond, Surrey TW9 1SR*

© Josie Metcalfe 1997

ISBN 0 263 80016 4

*Set in Times 10 on 11½ pt. by
Rowland Phototypesetting Limited
Bury St Edmunds, Suffolk*

03-9702-47802-D

*Printed and bound in Great Britain
by Mackays of Chatham PLC, Chatham*

CHAPTER ONE

'Does anyone else speak French?' Val called over the chaos of the overflowing accident department. It was Friday evening again and the rowdier element of the surrounding city seemed to have started early tonight.

'A little,' Tom Fletcher volunteered, and grimaced over his shoulder at her as he disappeared through the set of curtains to join a drunken reveller who mistakenly believed he could rival Pavarotti. 'Be with you as soon as I've finished in here.'

'Schoolgirl level only,' called Lily Balewa as she efficiently stripped the disposable paper sheet out of a newly vacated cubicle and replaced it with a fresh one. 'Why?'

'A small party of French tourists have been injured in a car accident. We won't know how good their English is until they get here, but I'd rather be prepared. . .'

'Sister?' An urgent voice broke into her explanation and she turned just in time to field the small child who was just about to cannon into her.

'And where do you think *you're* off to in such a hurry, sunshine?' Val swung the little dark-haired tornado into the air and she squealed with delight.

'Thanks, Sister,' the young nurse panted as she reached up to relieve her of her wriggling burden. 'This little monkey took off while I was helping her mum into a cubicle.'

'Better take her back before Mum gets worried, and

5

make sure she doesn't get away again—some of our customers aren't in a fit state to have her around.'

The sudden influx of paramedics and ambulance personnel escorting several laden stretchers drew her eyes to the next task.

'I hope you've lined up some interpreters,' Dick Trask warned as he prepared to hand over. 'They're too shocky to cope with anything other than their native tongue at the moment.'

'All organised,' Val reassured him with her fingers crossed out of sight. 'What have you got so far?'

'Four people in the car, average age approximately sixty. We think they forgot which side of the road they should be on when they came to a roundabout.'

'Nasty.' Val winced. 'How bad are the injuries?'

'Mostly cuts and bruises and shock, except for the oldest lady. She took the brunt of the impact on her side of the car.'

As they were speaking, Val had been directing the four into adjoining cubicles where the preliminaries would take place, making certain that Tom and Lily were available to translate the essential questions.

'*Madame?*' she began gently, her voice as reassuring as possible as she took the elderly lady's frail hand in hers. '*Je suis infirmière. Où avez-vous mal?*'

'*L'épaule et la hanche,*' came the whispered reply and the papery face screwed up in pain as she tried to point out which hip with her injured arm.

Val hid a smile when she understood the unladylike curse which emerged through the fiercely gritted teeth, and spared a brief thought for the unexpected use to which she was putting her hard-won French. Two years ago she'd been taking lessons towards the day of her long-awaited trip with Michael and. . .

She gave herself a mental shake. There was no time for travelling down that empty road. She had a patient to see to and, unless she had missed her mark, the poor woman was going to end up spending her holiday in hospital with a broken hip.

'*Il faut faire une radio,*' Val translated as she escorted her charge towards the X-ray department, then went on to explain that the plates were needed to see just how badly her hip had been injured before the orthopaedic surgeon could decide what sort of action to take.

'*Je dois téléphoner mon petit-fils,*' the patient suddenly announced, her words almost frantic. '*Puis-je téléphoner?*'

Why on earth did she want to phone her grandson? Val shrugged and succeeded in calming her down by promising to help her make the call as soon as the X-rays had been taken.

'*Monsieur. . .er. . .Guy?*' she began tentatively when the phone was answered at the other end and she suddenly realised that her patient had only given her his first name.

'*Oui?*' There was a slight hesitation before he answered but his voice, when it came, wasn't the light treble of a young Frenchman that she'd been expecting, but the slightly husky tenor of a fully adult male.

'*Il y a eu un accident. C'est votre grand-mère. . .*' She paused, racking her brain for the words to reassure him about his grandmother's condition, but when she'd decided to learn French she'd never expected to hold this sort of conversation. . .

'You are English?' The words were spoken as a question but the tone showed no hesitation. 'What has happened?'

Over her sigh of relief that she could revert to her own native tongue was the swift appreciation for the attractive Gallic accent which coloured his English.

'There was a car accident and your grandmother has a broken hip. She was most insistent that I should phone you so that she can speak to you before she goes into Theatre.'

'Is it possible for me to have a word with her surgeon as well? I'd like to know exactly what damage she has done and what he proposes doing about it.'

Val was a little taken aback by his sudden clipped demand, but in the circumstances there was no reason why he shouldn't be allowed to reassure himself that his grandmother was receiving the best of attention. And, anyway, she mentally excused him, he must be shocked by the news and hardly in a fit state to realise that he was being so abrupt.

'If you would like to have a word with your grandmother while I fetch him?' she suggested quietly before she handed the receiver over to his silvery-haired relative, propping it carefully on the pillow beside her head so that she didn't have to do any more than steady it with a hand already festooned with intravenous lines and identity bracelets.

Already the injections she'd been given to relieve the pain were working, but she was still very shaky as she murmured a loving greeting to the voice on the other end.

Val glanced down awkwardly at the watch pinned to the front of her uniform as she hurried along the corridor towards the surgical ward. One hand clutched her shopping bag and purse, while the other cradled the small posy of flowers she'd hastily purchased from the florist in the small arcade at the entrance to the hospital.

'Only fifteen minutes to the end of visiting time,' she muttered, remembering her intention to arrive at least half an hour earlier.

Unfortunately, it had taken longer than usual to sort out the chaos surrounding the last patient on her shift, with the young woman's father and her boyfriend almost coming to blows as they blamed each other for the fact that she'd taken an overdose of her mother's sleeping pills.

It was sheer luck that she'd been found fairly quickly and rushed into Casualty to have her stomach pumped out. Now it would be up to other branches of the medical profession to check on any residual effects of the drugs and to offer counselling to the poor girl to find out why she'd resorted to such drastic measures.

Val's heart was heavy with sympathy for all the people involved. She knew only too well that an outsider rarely saw the whole story behind a suicide attempt and she would always regret the fact that she hadn't seen the warning signs. . .

The guilt began to swamp her again, the way it always did when she thought about the events of two years ago.

Surely she should have realised how depressed Michael had become; should have guessed what he was planning. . .

If only he had spoken to her; had told her that he couldn't face. . .

'Oof. . .!' she gasped as she cannoned straight into the tall figure coming round the final bend in the corridor, and she found her arms grasped firmly in two hands as she teetered back on her sensible heels.

'Oh, I'm so sorry,' she said breathlessly as she took a step backwards, and his hands dropped away from

her. 'I'm afraid I wasn't looking where I was going. . .'
The words died away as she looked up over the open-
necked shirt, revealed by the open edges of a smartly
tailored suit, into a strikingly handsome face and she
was mesmerised by the wickedest pair of dark brown
eyes she had ever seen.

For several long seconds they gazed at each other in
silence, his eyes flickering over her face as she took in
the details of the thick dark hair falling haphazardly
over his forehead from a widow's peak and forming a
dark slash which nearly met the equally dark crescents
of his eyebrows.

The planes and hollows of his olive-toned cheeks
were framed by a closely trimmed beard and moustache
and, for the first time, Val found herself drawn to someone other than the clean-shaven men she usually
preferred.

Not that she was interested in *any* man these days,
and especially not some stranger she'd bumped into in
a hospital corridor.

She dragged her eyes away from his face and
side-stepped hurriedly, her cheeks flaming with embarrassment when she realised that she'd been standing
there staring at him. What on earth must he be thinking of her?

'I'm sorry,' she repeated huskily as she edged out of
his way and fixed her eyes on the doors to the ward.
'I'll get out of your way.'

'No problem,' she heard him murmur and the hint
of laughter in his voice made her face burn even hotter
as she scurried away from him.

What a fool she'd made of herself, staring at him like
that. Thank goodness she wasn't likely to see *him* again.

*   *   *

'Sister Burgess!' The elderly voice sounded so different now that Madame de Bourges was on the mend. There was no sign of a quaver as she greeted her visitor in perfect English. 'How kind of you to come up to see me!'

Val smiled as she laid the small posy of flowers she'd brought on top of the bedside cabinet beside the jug of water, and turned a chair round to face the bed.

'I just thought I'd pop in to see that you were doing all right, *madame*. The hospital grapevine told me that your friends were all released today to go back home and I didn't know whether you had any visitors, or needed someone to fetch anything for you.'

'Oh, but that is so kind of you,' she exclaimed. 'I'm sure you must be far too busy to waste your time over one old lady.'

'I must admit,' Val teased with a twinkle in her eye, 'if I'd known how good your English was, I wouldn't have been nearly so worried about you.'

'Oh! You must allow me to apologise for being so stupid when I was brought into the hospital. I was so confused that I quite forgot which country I was in. I was so grateful that there was someone who could understand me. . .' She reached out with her uninjured hand to grasp Val's, where it rested on the edge of the bed.

'I'm just glad that I was able to help. I can imagine how frightening it must have been.'

'Ah, but you must tell me. How does an English nurse come to speak such good French? Have you visited my country often or have you, perhaps, some French in your family?' She settled herself against the pile of pillows as though preparing for a long chat.

'No. There is no French blood in my family.' The

sharp stab of regret was swiftly ignored. 'And I haven't been to France—yet.'

'But you have been learning French so that you can visit soon?' she guessed, her dark eyes brightly inquisitive.

'We. . .' She hastily corrected herself. 'I had intended to visit Brittany and perhaps travel on into Normandy if I had time.'

'Ah, but this is a coincidence! I live in Rennes— the capital of Brittany. When you make your journey you must come to stay with me. . .'

Looking back on that conversation during her first visit to Madame de Bourges, Val remembered that she had made a noncommittal comment. She was certain that the invitation to visit had probably been no more than the usual politeness towards a chance acquaintance, and would soon be forgotten.

She had made the journey up to the orthopaedic ward several times, realising that the elderly lady would be rather lonely when the other patients in the ward were receiving visitors.

It was no hardship to spend time with her, the two of them finding that they shared similar tastes in music and literature—as well as a passion for tapestry and embroidery.

It was only in the dark loneliness of her room that Val could admit that she looked forward to the distraction of her visits every bit as much as their plucky patient, as the days of early February began to go past.

Once upon a time she had loved this time of year for the host of happy anniversaries which it brought—the Valentine's Day birthday which had prompted her parents to choose her name, her meeting, on her birthday, with the man who was to become her husband and their wedding exactly one year later. . .

No more!

It was nearly two years since all the good memories had been buried under sadness so that now she could hardly bear to think about her approaching birthday without feeling the depression begin to swamp her.

Last year she had tried to stay busy in an attempt at making the time go by faster but when the fateful day had arrived—with all the attendant teasing and nonsense among the staff in the department over anonymous Valentine's Day cards and the excitement over the annual Valentine's ball—she'd hated it.

And now, nearly a year later, she could see the date coming closer and closer on the calendar and dreaded a repeat of last year's unhappiness.

If only there was some way to avoid it, she thought hopelessly as she trudged up the last flight of stairs leading to the orthopaedic ward, contemplating the impossibility of taking a holiday somewhere abroad even at this time of year.

If only she had a fairy godmother who could wave a magic wand and take her away from all the memories—or, at least, make her fall asleep until Valentine's Day had gone by for another year.

The whimsical thought brought a wry expression to her face, which must have lingered as she approached the elderly lady's bed.

'You do not look very happy, *ma chère*. Is something the matter?' the softly accented voice demanded kindly. 'There is a problem with your work?'

'No.' Val determinedly shook off the grey cloud hovering over her head and found a more genuine smile.

'We've been busy but, with this icy weather, it's only to be expected.'

'Has it been very bad?' Madame demanded in some surprise, glancing towards the curtains drawn over the large windows down one side of the ward. 'It is so warm in the hospital that we don't really know what it's like outside.'

'You've probably noticed that there's been a lot of activity on the ward in the last day or so,' Val said.

'Yes. I noticed that all the empty beds have been filled, but I didn't think to wonder why. . .' She shrugged.

'There was a sudden freeze after the rain—' Val began.

'Ah! *Les collisions!*'

'There *were* some car crashes,' she agreed, 'but most of the injuries were due to people stepping onto icy patches and falling badly. In the space of six hours we've admitted twenty-seven people with broken legs and fifty-three with broken wrists.'

'*Oh! Les pauvres!*' Madame exclaimed. 'I can understand how they are feeling!' She grimaced pointedly at the bed.

'You were lucky, though. You were the only person to come in that evening needing surgery.'

'And this makes a difference?'

'A big difference because it will take about four hours in Theatre for each case, and with each surgeon working as fast as he can go, and each theatre going right around the clock with changes of staff, it will still mean that some people will be waiting for surgery for several days.'

'And that is without the others with broken wrists,

isn't it?' Madame added. 'I didn't realise how lucky I was!'

'You might be even luckier,' Val murmured as she leant closer. 'You've been making such good progress and the new patients will be needing beds, so. . .'

'Ah!' The dark eyes gleamed. 'You think there might be a chance that I could go home soon?'

Val raised one hand to show her fingers crossed for luck.

'It would depend on your situation at home, of course,' she cautioned. 'Your doctor would have to be willing to take over the supervision of your case and you. . . What?' she paused to demand when the elderly lady began to chuckle heartily.

'I am glad to say that this will not be a problem.' She laughed again. 'You have kindly visited me for several days now and I cannot believe that I did not tell you that my grandson lives with me.'

'Good.' Val smiled in response. 'Then he will be able to make all the arrangements for you to be checked by your own doctor.'

'But he *is* a doctor,' she spluttered with renewed humour. 'He will be able to keep a far closer eye on me than any hospital.'

Val joined in the laughter, but there was an element of sadness in it as she realised that she would soon be losing contact with the gallant Frenchwoman. She had grown quite attached to her and admired the determined way she had set her sights on a full recovery in the shortest possible time.

This could be the last time she was able to visit before her grandson arranged for her to be transferred to their home in Rennes. . .

'There it is again,' the elderly voice broke in, interrupting Val's thoughts. 'You do not look happy. What is it that you were thinking about?'

'I was just thinking that by tomorrow you might already be back in France, and I won't have anyone to visit.'

'Ah but why would you want to waste your time with an old woman?' Madame remonstrated. 'You have been so kind to sit and talk with me but a pretty girl like you must have all the handsome men waiting in a line. I hear the nurses talking about who will take them to the big dance and what they will wear.' She flicked a coquettish glance at Val. 'I expect you have a handsome man waiting to escort you. . .'

Val couldn't control the spasm of pain which flashed through her as the memories overwhelmed her in an avalanche.

'Oh, *ma chère*! What have I said?' One hand reached out to rest on Val's clenched white knuckles, the translucent skin paper-thin over the fragile bones. 'I am so sorry if I have hurt you. . .'

'No, *madame*. It's not your fault.' Val drew in a steadying breath and pushed the agony back down into the hidden dark corners of her soul. 'It's just. . . It's not a happy time of year for me.'

She straightened her shoulders and forced herself to meet the dark eyes full of questions and sympathy without flinching, forcing the words out through a throat grown tight with suppressed tears. 'Michael. . .my husband and my little son died on Valentine's Day,' she whispered.

'Val? Is that you?'

Tom Fletcher's voice accosted her from the corridor as she slid out of her coat and vainly tried to shake some of the rain off the shoulders before she hung it up. 'Message for you,' he continued.

'Hang on a minute, Tom. Hold your horses! Let me get my wet things off before you send me off on any errands.' She toed off each of her shoes and pushed them across the floor with wet, nylon-clad toes so that they rested under the radiator. With any luck they would be dry before she had to put them back on at the end of her shift.

'No errands,' the charge nurse said as he propped his lanky body against the doorframe to watch her rub a towel over her head, then apply it to her clammy feet. 'You're to go up to Orthopaedic as soon as you get in. Apparently it's something to do with the French woman we sent up there the other day.'

'Oh, Lord. There's nothing wrong with her, is there? She was doing so well when I saw her yesterday.' Val looked up at him from under her tousled hair with a worried gaze.

'No idea.' He shrugged and straightened to his full height. 'All I know is you're needed up there pronto.' He waved laconically and ambled out of sight.

Val shook her head. No one would think, to look at him, that he was one of the most experienced staff in the department and could move like greased lightning when the need arose.

'Pronto,' she muttered as she flicked a comb through the limp damp strands of her short dark hair. Thank goodness it had just enough natural curl so that it would dry in reasonable shape—if it got the chance.

If she'd just been going up to visit Madame de Bourges she would have made the effort to go up the stairs as part of her ongoing New Year's resolution to get fit.

Thank goodness she'd never really been overweight, she thought as she flattened herself against the side wall of the lift to allow a laden trolley to be manoeuvred in with her. But, with only just over a year to go until her thirtieth birthday, it made sense to start taking care of herself *before* she had a problem, and she was already noticing the difference in the fit of her uniforms.

'Sister Patterson? I had a message to come up as soon as I arrived,' Val reported formally when her knock brought an invitation to step into the office. 'Madame de Bourges hasn't had a set-back, has she?'

'No, Val. It's nothing like that. Just the reverse, in fact. We're hoping to release her to go back to France.'

'I see,' Val said as a puzzled frown pleated her forehead. 'Then what's this got to do with me, Patty?'

'Her release depends partly on you,' her colleague replied as she waved Val towards one of the chairs.

'On me?' Val's eyes opened wide as she paused in mid-stride then slid onto the seat.

'Yes. She's going to need medical assistance on the journey, and to hand over the responsibility to the medical services in her home town. She specially asked if you would be willing to accompany her in view of the fact that you speak excellent French.' Her eyebrows rose questioningly.

'Well, I wouldn't say it was excellent,' Val demurred as she felt the heat rise in her cheeks.

'It's bound to be a darned sight better than mine, so don't be modest,' 'Patty' Patterson quipped. 'Now, the only question is whether you're willing to go with her.'

'How long would I be away? I can hardly just take myself out of the duty roster and expect everyone else to cover for me.' The thoughts were whirling around in confusion inside her head. She'd longed for an excuse to get away from the hospital, but. . .

'How about taking some of your holiday entitlement?' Patty suggested. 'I know it's a rotten time of the year as far as the weather's concerned, but at least you'll be looking at French rain instead of English.'

'What. . .? How long. . .? Oh, God, I can't think straight!' Val shook her head in exasperation.

Patty laughed sympathetically.

'I had a quick word with the powers that be and they're quite happy for you to take up to ten days if necessary. You could minimise that if you tack some of your days off onto the end of it. Obviously, if you don't want to take that much time, or don't need it, you don't have to.'

'Ten days. . .?' Val did some quick mental calculations. That would take her well beyond the dreaded day of her birthday and all the other anniversaries and, with any luck, she would be so busy that she wouldn't even remember what the date was when it came. . . 'OK,' she nodded decisively, 'I'll take the full ten days. Should I have a word with Madame de Bourges?'

'Just slip into the ward and give her the good news.' Patty smiled. 'I think she's been sitting there with her fingers crossed ever since the suggestion came up. Her other option was to wait until her grandson was free to come over to collect her, and that could be several days.'

Val's head was still spinning as she approached their elderly patient's bed.

'You are coming to France with me? Yes?' she demanded eagerly as soon as she saw Val.

'Yes,' Val agreed with a smile. 'But I've no idea what the arrangements are—'

'*N'import*,' Madame interrupted with a dismissive

shrug. 'Guy will have done all those things for us. All that is necessary is for you to pack your *valise*.'

Val couldn't believe that it would be that simple, but when she returned to A and E she found that she had, indeed, been released with immediate effect and was informed that there would be an envelope of notes and instructions waiting for her when she returned to the hospital with her luggage that afternoon.

'I don't know whether I'm on my head or my heels,' she muttered as she stood in the middle of her tiny kitchen a couple of hours later and tried to think whether there was anything she'd forgotten to do.

'Plants have all gone next door with a spare key in case of emergencies,' she ticked off on her fingers. 'Note for the milkman, stop the newspapers, turn down the heating, put out the rubbish and do the last of the washing-up.' She turned in a circle as she gazed blankly around the room but nothing seemed out of place so she went through to the other rooms in turn.

'Nothing essential left behind in the bathroom and everything left clean and tidy,' she continued as she wandered into the bedroom. 'Underclothes, warm jumpers and shirts and trousers, nightwear, toiletries, footwear, make-up. . .'

She had a brief flash of memory as she remembered carefully folding the fine wool of her favourite burgundy-coloured dress. What on earth she thought she was going to be doing in France to need her most elegant dress was a mystery, but for some reason she'd found herself packing it.

She was just making a final sweep around her little sitting-room, with one eye on the time which was ticking away at an alarming rate, when she caught sight of the tapestry frame leaning against the arm of her chair and paused.

'Why not?' she said aloud as she grabbed the bag of different coloured wools and tucked them into the carrying bag she'd made for transporting it when she took it into work for her turns on night shift. 'It's not as if it weighs much, in spite of the fact it's a bit of an awkward shape. And who knows how much time I'll have to spend sitting about waiting for the rain to stop?'

She gathered up the straps and handles of her small collection of luggage, the weight of the suitcase reminding her of the thick folder of papers and notes she'd added at the last minute. This might not be the trip to France that she and Michael had planned but, as she was actually going to the very region they had intended to visit, who knew what time she might have to look at old parish records and suchlike?

'How are you feeling?' Val questioned gently as she reached across for her patient's wrist. 'Do you need any more pain relief?'

'No, no. I'm fine,' the softly accented voice reassured her with a beatific smile. 'I'm so pleased to be going home that there's no room inside me for anything but happiness!'

'What a pity we can't bottle that feeling. You could be a very wealthy woman!' Val teased as she noted down the figures on the chart.

They were on the last stage of their journey now, in a specially adapted private ambulance which was speeding them effortlessly through the darkness of the early evening.

Their transfer from the hospital to a chartered flight had been just the first of several surprises for Val, but her patient's easy acceptance made her wonder just what sort of life she usually led if such treatment went without comment.

She knew from their conversations during her visits to the orthopaedic ward that her patient had been a widow for several years but had learnt only yesterday that her grandson was a doctor.

Even so, unless the rates of pay for the profession were wildly different between the two countries facing each other across the English channel, she was at a loss to know how a mere doctor had been able to arrange— and afford—such first-rate service at such short notice.

Still, she admonished herself, it was really none of her business. She was just supposed to be taking care of Madame de Bourges until she was safely settled in her own home and under the care of her own physician.

She'd been persuaded to accept the offer of accommodation in the de Bourges household, but had every intention of removing herself at the earliest moment.

She enjoyed the elderly lady's company but knew that once she was returned to her beloved grandson her need for Val's attention would disappear. It would make the situation easier all round if she used her original intention to explore the region as the reason to leave their hospitality.

After all, she reminded herself, who knew how long it would be before she had a chance to return to France?

'We're here!' Madame de Boruges's happy voice broke into Val's musings as the luxurious vehicle drew to a halt in front of double wooden doors with a security light gleaming brightly down onto the short flight of stone steps leading up to them. 'Oh, it's so good to be home!'

As Val peered out of the car windows to try to catch

a glimpse of the house in the surrounding darkness one of the doors opened to release a broad swathe of golden light down the steps and right across the car, almost like a bright welcoming carpet.

A tall dark figure was silhouetted briefly in the doorway before he stepped swiftly towards them and reached for the doorhandle.

'*Guy. Mon chèr!*' The frail hand Madame offered was grasped between two lean palms and drawn upwards for a gentle kiss. 'Grand-mère... *Bienvenue*,' a husky voice said before its owner leant a little further into the vehicle and dark eyes gleamed brilliantly across at Val in the subdued light. '*Bienvenue, mademoiselle*. Welcome to our home.'

Val was stunned into silence, her tongue paralysed and her breath non-existent as she recognised the darkly tanned, bearded face of the man she'd cannoned into in the corridor at the hospital.

CHAPTER TWO

'Isn't he handsome?' Madame demanded as Val helped her to don an exquisitely embroidered and pin-tucked nightdress, ready for her first night back in her own bed.

'Of course, *madame*,' Val replied with a smile. 'How could a grandson of yours be anything other than handsome?'

'Pah!' she exclaimed in disgust. 'I don't need flattery at my age. I prefer honesty.' Her dark eyes, so like those of the man in question, bored fiercely into Val's. 'Perhaps you prefer blond hair and blue eyes?' she suggested with a hint of scorn.

'No, *madame*,' Val replied quietly. 'I like dark-haired men well enough. My husband had dark hair and dark eyes much like your grandson.'

'Oh!' One frail hand covered her mouth penitently. 'I am so sorry, *ma chère*, I had quite forgotten. Will you forgive a foolish old woman?'

'Only if you promise to settle down and go straight to sleep,' Val replied sternly. 'Otherwise I will be forced to take drastic measures.'

The smile she forced to her lips must have seemed like the real thing to her elderly patient as she relaxed immediately and closed her eyes obediently.

Val turned to retrieve the tray she'd set aside after the light meal they'd eaten together and she released the breath she'd been holding.

It must be tiredness which was making her overreact like this. She didn't usually feel so vulnerable just at the thought of Michael's colouring, and she'd never panicked at the thought of sharing a meal with a colleague before.

Her cheeks heated at the memory of the way she'd hastily turned down Guy's offer of dinner in the dining-room after she'd settled his grandmother for the night, in favour of keeping the old lady company while she ate her own meal.

Had either of her French hosts noticed that just the thought of spending time in Guy's company had made her pulse begin to race and her palms grow clammy?

She balanced the tray on one palm as she pulled the door open quietly, then nearly dropped the whole thing when a husky voice broke into her thoughts.

'Is she asleep?' Guy lifted the tray from her precarious grasp and instantly the quivering chatter of cutlery on fine china ceased.

'I think so,' Val murmured with a quick glance back over her shoulder into the dimly lit room. 'She was so pleased to be home that she didn't want to go to sleep, but I think the journey made her tired enough to give her no option.'

'And you?' he questioned softly as she drew the door closed. 'Are you too tired to join me for a cup of coffee or a glass of brandy?'

Once again Val was mesmerised by the wicked expression in his dark eyes. She realised only too well that he had issued her a challenge.

Suddenly, for the first time in nearly two years, she felt a stirring of the adventurous spirit which had once been such an important part of her character.

'Tired, but not too tired,' she replied, and was pleased to catch a glimpse of surprise on his face before he controlled it.

'Good,' he said with a brief nod of acknowledgement. 'Follow me while I put this in the kitchen, then we'll go through to the fire.'

'I'm glad you don't expect me to be able to find my own way,' Val murmured wryly as she followed him down a different staircase. 'I think I'd get lost and still be wandering around at breakfast-time.'

He chuckled briefly.

'It's not really as bad as it seems,' he said as he turned to push a door open with his shoulder, and Val found herself in a kitchen big enough to swallow up the whole of her little flat with ceilings high enough for two rooms.

'It's very simple, really,' he continued as he put the tray down. 'There is the big staircase you went up when you first arrived. That goes up the centre of the house, with half of the rooms on each side. Then, at each end of the house there is a smaller set of stairs. One leads down this side to the kitchen and the other is on my side of the house and leads from my bedroom to my study.'

He turned to smile at her, his teeth very white against his olive skin and the closely trimmed dark hair of his beard as he pulled the door open and stood aside for her.

'Is the house very old?' Val asked, her voice annoyingly breathless as she walked past him and suddenly became aware of the woody scent of the soap he used.

'As far as we can trace it was built about two hundred years ago, after the big fire in Rennes.'

'Did your family build it?' Val had been fascinated by the history of the region as soon as she had started researching it and to find herself staying in such an historic house was a bonus.

'No. We've only been here for ninety years.'

'Really? You're wearing your years well,' she said,

barely managing to keep a straight face at the look of
surprise in his eyes before he realised that she was
teasing.

'Well,' he began with a wicked glint, 'it's a very
healthy region and we generally live to a ripe old age.'
The smile became a full-fledged grin, and Val was
almost certain she saw the hint of a pair of matching
dimples half-hidden in the closely cropped beard covering his cheeks.

A brief pang clutched at her heart as she remembered
another pair of dimples on a smoothly shaven face but
she pushed the memory away. There would be enough
time in the next ten days for her to think about Michael
when there was no one with her to notice the pain that
his going had left her suffering.

Perhaps this trip would be the means of finally laying
it all to rest; of letting go of all the anger and despair. . . .

'Your grandmother is certainly a good example,' she
offered, hastily directing the conversation away from
her thoughts, as she settled herself into a deliciously
comfortable chair on one side of the blazing fire. 'Her
progress has been phenomenal.'

'She's a very determined woman,' he agreed, smiling
fondly. 'She never accepts anything less than maximum
effort from herself or anyone around her until a job
is done—and that includes getting back on her own
two feet!'

'She certainly put the physiotherapist through his
paces at the hospital,' Val told him. 'Usually, after a
big operation like that, patients try to get him to treat
them gently and easily, but she was insisting that he
take her through the exercises "just one more time"
until I think he was more exhausted than she was!'

'Typical!' he snorted as he leaned over her to hand

her the glass of brandy she had chosen. 'I'm afraid that's going to be part of your job—making sure she doesn't do too much too soon for her own good.'

'Oh, but. . .' Val frowned in puzzlement, not certain that she had heard correctly or whether the brief contact of his lean fingers against hers as he handed her the cool glass had short-circuited her brain. 'I was told you'd managed to arrange for a physiotherapist to visit her here.'

'I have, but she'll only be here for an hour each morning five days a week, and even though Berthe is here every day doing the housekeeping she can't be expected to keep an eye on Grand-mère all the time.'

Val could see the logic in what he was saying, but it certainly wasn't what she had expected to happen when she'd agreed to accompany the elderly lady to France.

'But how long would you be wanting me to stay?' she said hesitantly, a strange feeling of uncertainty creeping over her at the thought of spending too much time in the company of this dark-eyed charmer.

'When do you have to be back at work? I understood your hospital was giving you some of your holiday entitlement immediately.'

'They have. But I was thinking of doing some exploring around the area and. . .'

'And I'm being very selfish in expecting you to give up your precious holiday time to play gaoler for my grandmother,' he completed gruffly. 'I'm sorry. Of course you won't want to sit with her while she does her tapestry and chatters on about her memories. She's my responsibility and it's up to me to keep her occupied while she heals.'

'How will you manage?' Val asked quietly, knowing

it really wasn't any of her business but haunted by an
inexplicable feeling that she was somehow letting him
down. 'How can you spend time with her *and* fulfil
your duties at the hospital?'

'God knows, especially as Mireille's on maternity
leave and we're short-handed at the moment,' he said
tiredly as he ran the fingers of both hands through his
hair, to leave it standing up in endearingly ruffled
spikes, before dragging his palms down and scrubbing
them over his face.

Even though she was sitting on the other side of the
crackling fire, Val could hear the sound of his beard
against his hands and wondered if the closely trimmed
dark hair would be bristly or silky to the touch.

She found herself clenching her fingers into fists
against the tingling she felt at the wayward thought.

'How about a compromise?' she heard herself sug-
gest and could have bitten her tongue with vexation.

'What are you suggesting?' His dark eyes were fixed
intently on her so that she knew that there was no way
she could take back the words. What a fool she was!
If she hadn't spoken, she could have said goodbye to
this disturbing man in the morning and been on her
way. Now. . .

'Well, I was hoping to be able to do some sightseeing
in the area to see if I could trace some old. . .family
connections.'

'And?'

'I was thinking that Rennes is fairly central to the
area I wanted to explore and if we could work out some
sort of timetable. . .'

'You'd be willing to sacrifice a proportion of your
time to nail Grand-mère's foot to the floor?' he queried
hopefully.

'Something like that,' Val chuckled. 'After all, I can't spend all day looking at dusty old pieces of paper.'

'Oh, thank you. A thousand times! I've been so worried that she might try to do too much and re-injure herself before she's completely healed.'

'Well, I promise that, while she's in my care, I won't let her go climbing any trees or taking up hang-gliding.'

'Don't joke about it!' He looked alarmed. 'Sometimes I dread coming home because I never know what she's up to!'

It was early evening the next day before Val saw Guy again. She and Madame de Bourges had spent a very companionable day together, most of the time in the same chairs and in front of the same fire she'd shared with Guy last night.

As yet Val hadn't regretted her decision to stay because the weather was dull, wet and windy, while the house was a haven of cosy comfort.

'Don't tell me she's twisted your arm into doing some of her interminable stitchery!' a familiar husky voice exclaimed as he entered the room, one hand tugging at the knot of his tie until it had slid far enough down for him to open the first two buttons on his shirt.

For several seconds Val's eyes were mesmerised by the tantalising glimpse of dark hair in the V of white fabric and she had to drag them away to focus on the lightweight frame resting on her lap.

'Not at all,' she began in a breathless voice. 'This one is all my own,' and she stood it upright and turned it to face him so that he could see the picture forming under her needle. It was no coincidence that all he would see of her was her eyes. At least that way she had a chance to regain her composure.

Dear God, what was happening to her? The last time her pulse had beat this fast was when Michael had asked her out for the first time. . .

She watched silently as he walked towards her, his dark eyes travelling over the half-completed representation of a Dutch painting.

'I recognise that,' he said, sounding quite delighted.

'The *Arnolfini Marriage Group* by Jan van Eyck,' Val told him.

'I really like that. It's so much better than interminable bunches of flowers and bowls of fruit,' he said with a pointed grin in his grandmother's direction.

'Horrible child!' she scolded. 'You know very well they are replacements for the worn-out seats in the dining-room. They were supposed to look like a set. Anyway,' she said with a scowl, 'you will be pleased to hear that this is the very last one. The next tapestry will be a new firescreen to go in front of this fire in the summer. I was thinking of doing a large vase of flowers about the same size as the piece Valentine is working on.'

'More flowers!' he groaned, quite missing the wicked sparkle in her eye as she winked at Val.

Val laughed aloud. '*Madame*, you are a terrible tease!'

'Won't you call me Simone, please?' she suggested gently. 'It is much more friendly.'

'But it doesn't feel right,' Val demurred uncomfortably, flicking a quick glance at Guy to gauge his reaction.

'Then you must call her Grand-mère, as I do,' he pronounced. 'Then we shall all be relaxed with each other.'

Val didn't comment, but she doubted that she would

ever feel relaxed in his presence. He was such a dynamic man that the air almost seemed to quiver around him, his dark good looks the epitome of the stereotypical tall, dark and handsome.

She really didn't understand what was happening to her. For the last two years her heart and her emotions had been encased in ice and she had believed that nothing would ever melt them. Now, with just the dark intensity of his gaze, Guy de Bourges seemed to have reached inside the frozen wastes and started a slow thaw.

'Tomorrow morning I will take you into Rennes to do some sightseeing,' he announced from his position at the head of the table as the three of them finished the delicious meal Berthe had served before she left for her own home.

'But what about your grandmother?' Val glanced across at the elegant figure sitting perfectly upright at the other side of the table. 'She will be all alone once the physiotherapist leaves.'

'Ah, no, my dear. I will be having visitors,' she announced with a smile.

'Well, then——' Val bit her lip, realising that she would be intruding if she was to stay '——I would be grateful if I could have a lift into Rennes tomorrow. I am sure I can find my own way back if you will tell me what time your visitors will be leaving.'

'Silly child,' Madame de Bourges said fondly. 'The visitors have been arranged by Guy to keep an eye on me so that you may have some time to relax. You mustn't feel that you are intruding. I want you to treat our house as your own while you are here.'

Val fixed her eyes on the firelight gleaming in the

last drop of wine in her glass as she felt the heat rise in her cheeks. 'Thank you, *madame*, but I wouldn't want to take advantage of your hospitality—'

'Hospitality? Nonsense!' Guy broke in. 'We are both indebted to you for giving up your time to keep an eye on this disobedient wretch. *We* are the ones taking advantage of *you*, so let's not hear any more about it. Can you be ready to leave at half past eight?'

Val murmured her assent, grateful when his grandmother drew his attention away with her declaration that it was time for her to go to her room.

As soon as possible Val escaped to her own room, closing the heavy door to cross the deep-pile carpet and slump into the wing chair beside the heavily draped window.

Ten days! However was she going to cope with ten days in his company, even intermittently, when she felt as if her every nerve was hyper-sensitive to his presence.

What was it about Guy de Bourges that fascinated her?

Granted, he had the same colouring and a similar build to the only man she had ever fallen in love with, but her initial attraction to Michael had never been as intense as this. And, remembering the pain her love for Michael had eventually brought her, why hadn't the similarity acted as a deterrent to her fascination?

Now she was reduced to hiding away in her room when she was far from ready to go to sleep, just so that she wouldn't be tempted to spend the evening in his company in front of the fire.

She scowled crossly as she flounced under the covers, having taken twice as long as necessary to get ready for bed just to help the time pass.

She'd left her tapestry downstairs and nothing would

induce her to go down to retrieve it in case she bumped into Guy. She had definitely spent all the time she could cope with in his company today.

So, unless she wanted to torment herself with starting one of the romantic novels she'd brought with her, that just left the folder of information she'd gathered to read through.

Slowly she leafed through the pages of notes she'd begun making once she'd started her research.

It was Michael who'd started her off, of course. His story of the family connection with the Huguenots who'd fled persecution in France in the sixteenth century to settle in England had captured her imagination.

It hadn't taken much persuasion on his part to get her to begin the long and painstaking task of tracing the generations back to establish connections with surviving members of the same families in France—especially as neither of them had any living relatives of their own.

She stifled the sharp pain which came as she reached the small group of photographs and tried to remember the laughter when she'd put them in the folder.

'That one's my father,' Michael had said as he handed her a slightly fuzzy photo of a handsome gentleman wearing plus fours and a knitted pullover. 'And this one was my grandfather.' The ragged-edged print showed a gentleman in a frock coat holding a top hat.

She lined the two old photos up beside the more modern one of Michael and marvelled again at how startlingly alike all three faces were. If it weren't for the different hairstyles and the age of the photos they could easily be taken for the same man.

The last face she added to the line was a far younger one with cheeks still bearing the chubbiness of babyhood, but the likeness was still unmistakable. Simon.

Her precious baby. When that photo had been taken he had been the latest link in an unbroken chain.

Val drew in an unsteady breath as she forced her thoughts away from her loss and remembered instead the way she'd teased Michael.

'Aren't you worried that we might find another branch of your family still thriving in France?' she'd said. 'Perhaps I'll meet a sexy Frenchman who looks just like you!'

She smiled as she'd remembered the way he'd pretended to be outraged that she could think of replacing him and they'd compromised by saying that she could bear Michael's mythical French twin in mind in case anything ever happened to him.

'Well, Michael,' she murmured as she stroked one finger gently over his face in the photo. 'I finally made it to France, but I haven't found your twin yet.' Guilt swamped her as the next words leapt into her mind, making her feel totally disloyal that she should be acknowledging how sexy Guy was while she was touching Michael's photo, and she hastily shuffled the papers together and slid them back into the file.

Once she was lying in the dark it wasn't quite so easy to silence the little voice inside her head. It was perfectly true that she hadn't found Michael's twin—she hadn't even started checking the places she'd listed to trace the branches of his family. But it was also undeniable that Guy was the first man who had sparked her interest since Michael's death and, disloyal or not, she just happened to find him the sexiest man she'd ever met in her life.

'If we're lucky this rain might ease up in a little while, so what do you want to see first?' Guy demanded when he directed his silver Citroën out of the driveway towards Rennes town centre.

'Church records and archives,' Val replied promptly, the precious file held securely on her lap and a notebook and pencil ready in her handbag.

'Good Lord!' He sounded stunned. 'What on earth for? I thought you wanted to go sightseeing.'

'That, too,' she conceded. 'But this trip has been planned for a long time. I'm trying to find out if there are any surviving members of the French branch of the family living in this area.'

'Under what name?' It sounded as if Guy's interest had been caught. 'Perhaps I'll have heard of them and can short-circuit your search.'

'I'm not certain, exactly, because a lot of the French names were Anglicised over the years. One of the books I've researched takes the name Burgess back to the middle of the eighteen-hundreds and suggests it's a corruption of the word *bourgeois*.'

'Not very helpful,' he agreed. 'Any other clues?'

'Another source suggests that there might be a connection with a family originating in the Bordeaux region who, when they arrived in London, apparently had some connection with the name de Goussec or de Goussey— but that part of the story was handed down as a verbal tradition so I've no idea of the true spelling.'

'You've set yourself quite a task,' he said wryly.

'It's worse than you think. Apparently, there was a sister who had some connection with the group of refugees who settled in Norwich, but I haven't had a chance to research that angle at all yet.'

'Have you anything else to go on as far as the French end of your search is concerned?'

'Nothing tangible,' she admitted, knowing that she

could never tell him about her joke with Michael about the quest for his twin. It had been all right to tease each other about what she would do in the event of his death when it seemed as if it was an event in the distant future.

Anyway, there was no guarantee that the strong family likeness between the members of Michael's family came from the Huguenot side at all.

In fact, if she was honest with herself, she would have to admit that, although her enthusiasm for tracing Michael's Huguenot ancestors was as keen as ever, she was suddenly finding it hard to drum up any interest in a mythical man, who may or may not resemble him, when every nerve in her body was aware only of the man sitting next to her in the close confines of his car.

'So, how did you know to come to *this* area of France?' Guy asked, in between pointing out the university buildings through the dismal weather and indicating the general direction of the hospital where he worked.

'It wasn't easy, believe me,' Val said with feeling, remembering the many hours of poring over dusty old books and documents and old church records and the weeks spent waiting for replies to letters of enquiry.

'Because the exodus of Huguenots had virtually finished by the middle of the eighteenth century, I first had to trace the family line back beyond that point to establish a clear link with Huguenots in England.'

'Then, I suppose, you had to work back the other way once you had some names and areas of origin in France?' he suggested.

'Exactly. But, with the Anglicisation of names and the way the Huguenots had to move about to escape persecution, I've ended up with several possibilities to trace. It was the trail that started off in the Bordeaux region that led me to this area.'

As she said the words Val marvelled how few of them it took to cover the months of effort it had taken to get that far.

'I'd always understood that there was a greater concentration of Huguenots in Normandy,' he murmured in an aside as they waited in a queue of traffic, his fingers tapping lightly on the steering-wheel in counterpoint to the rain falling on the roof of the car.

'There was, towards the end of the seventeenth century—more than ten times the number in Brittany—but my strongest lead told me to try Rennes first, so when I got the chance to spend some time here. . .' She shrugged.

'So, where exactly do you want to start?'

'Can you direct me to the Museé de Bretagne? I was told there's a wonderful collection of documents there and I was promised that they're presented logically and clearly.'

He chuckled and the sound filled the enclosed space around them. 'You said that with feeling. I take it some of the information has been difficult to unearth?'

'Difficult? Make that ''nearly impossible'' and you'd be closer to the truth. One example is birth certificates. French ones carry a lot more information than English ones—thank God—but I've found English information about deaths and burial dates is better than French.'

'Not exactly the sort of national information that's general knowledge,' he commented with a laugh as he drew to a halt among the puddles in the car park outside the museum.

'Here we are,' he announced as he leant forward to switch off the engine and then reached for his doorhandle. 'And, if we get bogged down with paperwork

on the ground floor, we can always go upstairs and
have a look at the collection of European art.'

'We. . .?' Val paused as she reached for the catch of
her seat belt. 'Oh, no. I didn't mean for you to waste
your time over this. I'm sure you've got much more
important things to do. Aren't you on duty at the
hospital?'

He looked back at her over his shoulder, one foot
already out of the open door as he changed his mind
and reached back into the car for the umbrella on the
floor behind his seat.

'No. I'm free until later this afternoon,' he informed
her with a cheerful smile. 'Of course I've brought my
pager with me in case of emergencies but, until then,
my time's my own.'

'But. . .'

'But nothing,' he said firmly. 'I've decided it's time
I learnt a little more about the history of my own region,
so lead on. . .' And he ducked his head under the lintel
and straightened to his feet as he opened out the
umbrella.

Val blew out an exasperated sigh.

It was bad enough when she was in the de Bourges
house, never knowing when Guy would appear, but
she'd thought at least she would have been able to
restore her equilibrium with a sojourn among old
documents. Now he was even going to invade her
solitude there.

As he locked the car she tucked the precious folder
inside her coat and wrapped both arms around it to
clutch it closely against her body as he offered to share
the shelter.

They set off in the direction of the entrance, their
shoulders rubbing together at each step as he angled

the umbrella to deflect most of the rain away from the two of them.

She was here to do research, she lectured herself sternly as she entered the impressive building and gratefully drew a deep breath as she stepped away to put a little distance between them.

Guy would probably want to wander about, looking at the various historic exhibits, and, as far as she was concerned, the more distance he put between them the better. But in any case she was determined that she wasn't going to let him disturb her concentration.

In the event, in spite of her whispered protestations, he stayed with her and turned out to be a great help, halving the time it would have taken for her to check whether the records held there had the information she wanted.

'So, you aren't any further forward in your search,' he commiserated as she finally admitted defeat.

'Well, if I was looking on the bright side I'd say that I'd just eliminated one of the places on my list, but if I'm honest they didn't have any of the sort of information I was looking for.'

'In that case, I think we ought to console ourselves with a visit to a little restaurant I know,' he declared with a smile as he held the heavy door open for her, the umbrella ready for her to step under. 'They serve the most amazing dishes and all of them made with local ingredients.'

Val's heart gave a silly leap at the thought that he wanted to prolong their time together, then squashed it firmly. The poor man had just spent hours being bored to death. He must be starving.

'And what would you have suggested if we'd been

wildly successful and tracked down the last piece of information?'

'That we needed to celebrate our success, of course,' he said, looking down at her through the shadows under the umbrella with a wicked grin.

'Of course,' Val echoed wryly, and nodded her thanks when he unlocked the car door for her.

He was just fastening his own seat belt when a sharp bleeping sound filled the car, and he swore softly as he reached for the mobile phone fitted to the console.

The conversation which followed was so fast that Val was barely able to follow more than the gist of it, in spite of her efforts to learn French. Even so, she knew that the situation was bad.

'I'm sorry,' he muttered as he hung up the receiver and reached forward to the ignition almost simultaneously. 'I'll have to drop you off at the nearest taxi rank and leave you to make your own way back to the house. There's been a crash and I'll have to go.'

'Out at the airport. I heard,' Val confirmed. 'How many injured?'

'Two families in a light aircraft,' he detailed as he wove as swiftly through the traffic as the heavy rain would allow. 'The pilot misjudged his landing in the poor visibility and there are children injured.'

'In that case, you needn't think that you're dumping me at the side of the road to get wet while I wait for a taxi when I can come with you. An extra pair of hands will always come in useful.'

He flicked her a swift glance, his eyes scanning her face as though he could read her sincerity there, then, as though satisfied with what he saw, he returned his full concentration back to the road with a brief nod. 'If you're certain that's what you want, thanks for the offer,' he said quietly as he followed the signs for the airport.

CHAPTER THREE

GUY's silver Citroën was obviously well known.

They'd hardly slowed down at the entrance to the restricted area of the airfield before the policeman on duty recognised him and waved him on in the direction of the crash.

'Oh, Lord!' Val murmured as she caught sight of the stricken plane for the first time.

Surrounded by the airport emergency vehicles with their lights strobing the scene, it looked like a mortally injured bird, collapsed onto its side with one broken wing sticking up towards the sky and half the tail-plane in tatters like bedraggled feathers across the sodden grass.

The two of them exited the car simultaneously as he drew to a halt at the nearest edge of the runway and, pausing only to grab his essential bag, Guy's long legs soon caught up with Val as she reached the group of rescuers.

'How can I help?' Val demanded as soon as Guy had been briefed, hating to stand idle in the face of such tragedy.

'Can you help with setting up a triage area? At the moment, as they bring out the passengers they're taking them straight to the ambulance over there without checking the severity of the injuries first. I need to establish which of the victims require immediate treatment.'

While he spoke he handed Val the inevitable

disposable gloves and snapped a pair on his own hands
with practised ease.

Val nodded her agreement and sped towards the mill-
ing group around the airport ambulance, recognising
that among the official crew there were a number of
civilian volunteers.

Once again she found herself blessing her efforts at
learning French as she introduced herself to the crew
of the ambulance, and offered to assist the volunteers
to set out the stretchers and equipment in the clear area
between the frantic activity surrounding the shattered
plane and the rescue vehicles.

Suddenly there was an air of purpose in the disparate
group as each was given a task with clear orders as to
how it should be performed. Within minutes there was
a row of stretchers laid out, each one rapidly acquiring
an occupant.

Bystanders were pressed into service to hold blankets
over the victims to shelter them from the continuing
rain while Guy assessed the severity of their condition
and assigned their order of importance.

A couple of times Val saw the surprise on a civilian's
face when an apparently horrendous flesh wound was
all but ignored. She knew that, in this first round of
triage, Guy would be checking only for the principal
immediate threats to life.

As horrendous as it might initially seem to a
bystander, salvage of a life would always take pre-
cedence over the salvage of a limb, and in order that
triage might accomplish the greatest good for the greatest number, it might even be necessary to bypass
completely those who were hopelessly injured.

As Guy moved swiftly from patient to patient, Val
assisted by tagging each of them with a colour-coded

label containing a brief record of essential information
and then assigning assistants to begin immediate treatment. Her task was considerably eased by the arrival
of the first of the ambulances from the hospital and the
influx of more trained personnel.

Guy had quickly established that none of the victims
rescued so far were in danger of dying from asphyxia
or haemorrhage.

Soon he and Val were supervising and directing the
setting up of a veritable forest of IV drips and the
application of emergency splints and dressings to various of the injured to stabilise them preparatory to
loading them into the ambulances. Suddenly there were
two simultaneous calls, one from the front of the plane
and the other from one of the stretchers.

'You take the patient on the stretcher; I'll go to the
plane,' Guy directed as he slogged his way through the
increasingly muddy grass.

The paramedic dealing with a nearly hysterical
woman, spattered with blood from a scalp wound, was
quick to tell Val that once all the victims had been seen
in the triage area a head count had revealed that there
was one child missing—possibly still trapped inside
the plane.

Val wiped her wet face on the sleeve of her coat to
hide her instant dismay, her throat closing in sympathy
as she peered through the continuing downpour towards
the crumpled aircraft to see Guy talking to one of the
emergency fire crews and gesturing towards the plane.

'I think they've found someone,' she said, reaching
for the woman's hand and squeezing it reassuringly.
Her cautious heart began to hope as she watched the
tall figure crouch down to reach in carefully through
the shattered windscreen.

She only realised that she'd automatically spoken in French when the poor woman replied in the same language, demanding tearfully that Val go over to see if her child was safe.

'Guy?' she called as she approached the tight knot of people grouped around the nose of the plane. 'Have you found the missing child?'

Suddenly there was an ominous silence and the group parted as Guy straightened up and turned sharply to face her.

'Child? What child? We were told they were all accounted for.'

Val's heart sank like a stone as she gestured over her shoulder towards the distressed woman. 'She's only just realised that there's one missing and. . . If you haven't found. . . Who's still in there?' she demanded, her mind processing facts faster than her tongue could voice them.

'The pilot. He's trapped. Initially we thought he was dead so he was left till last,' Guy detailed succinctly.

'Can you get him out?'

'Not without cutting the plane open.' He gestured towards the heavy cutting gear the fire crew were positioning at the scene, ready to begin work as soon as the paramedics had done their best to stabilise the injured man. 'And now we daren't start in case this child's still alive inside and the movement does more damage.'

'Will the pilot survive the delay while you look for the child?' Val demanded as they all circled the plane and peered in through the various holes and windows in an attempt to catch sight of the missing child.

Guy gave an expressive shrug and Val's heart sank. If the child died while they tried to rescue the pilot it would be a replay of her worst nightmares. The emergency services hadn't even realised that Simon was in the car with Michael until it was too late to save him. If only they had. . .

'The child must be trapped inside somewhere.' Guy's voice broke into her fruitless replay of that fateful crash. 'We got the rest out through the co-pilot's door because the whole fuselage was twisted by the impact and the seats were blocking the other door.'

'So no one's seen the child since the crash?' She absent-mindedly wiped at the rain which ran down her nose in a steady stream.

'Neither sight nor sound,' he confirmed. 'It could mean that it didn't survive the crash. . .'

'Or was knocked unconscious,' Val offered hopefully, subduing a shudder of revulsion as her eyes went towards the mangled rear section of the flimsy-looking plane.

'Either way, we can't make contact because of the impossible access. There's only that gash in the side of the plane.' He pointed to the ragged aperture behind the last window. 'It's too small for any of the rescue team to get through and they won't be able to enlarge it without endangering the pilot.'

'But—' Val broke off in frustration, her eyes fixed on the narrow gap.

'Anyway, there's no guarantee that the child would be accessible inside. The side of the cabin has collapsed inwards and made the space too small.'

'How small?' Val challenged, determination making her chin rise in spite of the fear cramping her stomach. 'Too small for a child to crawl through or too small for an adult male?' As she fired the questions at him she was stripping her bulky coat off, and he was so surprised when she flicked it towards him that he caught it.

'Hey! What do you think you're doing?' he demanded belatedly, as she put one hand on the ragged
opening in the side of the small plane, and he grabbed
her shoulder.

'Waiting for a leg-up,' she said calmly, her chin lifting another notch as she met his gaze. 'If I can get
inside without making the plane shift I can look for
the child.'

'No!' he said fiercely, his dark eyes intense. 'Leave
it to the emergency services. It's too dangerous for you
to go climbing about in there.'

'It's too dangerous for a child to be in there too,' she
reminded him softly, one hand coming to rest on his
forearm in entreaty. 'I'll go slowly and I won't take
any chances, but I couldn't live with myself if I
didn't try...'

She turned her eyes resolutely upwards, peering
through the falling rain to fix her gaze on the darkness
beyond the gaping hole in the side of the plane. Subduing a shudder, she clenched her teeth against her
instinctive fear.

Now was not the time to remember how much she
hated being in confined places; there was a child in
there, injured and possibly dying, who needed her help.

Guy called out something to one of the drenched
rescuers who argued vociferously as he approached—
obviously horrified at the thought of a civilian risking
her life in such a way—until Val turned her head and
stared straight at him, her determination absolute.

Suddenly he capitulated, his expression sombre as he
worked out with Guy how they could best help her to
get inside.

Between them they lifted her off the ground and
supported her weight as she felt carefully around inside

the opening for a suitable area to climb onto, the steady downpour soaking her fine wool shirt as she began to thread herself through the jagged edges and into the dimness of the interior head first.

'What a mess,' she muttered through teeth clenched tight with fear as she inched her way through the debris and into the sharply tilted chaos of what was left of the central passageway. 'Any idea where the child was sitting?' she called back over her shoulder.

She heard the demand repeated outside in spite of the sound of the heavy rain striking the outside of the fuselage and waited for a reply, her eyes busy all the while searching the gloom for any sign of movement.

'The child is a five-year-old boy called Laurent and he was sitting next to one of the right-hand windows,' Guy's voice called through the hole behind her and, resisting the frantic urge to crawl back to him as fast as she could, Val began to worm her way carefully forward.

There was an ominous creaking and groaning as the plane suddenly shifted and she froze, barely hearing the shouts of warning outside as terror swept over her that her weight might make the plane tip right over and trap her alive in a tomb.

'Laurent,' she called, her voice thready as she forced the word out through lips drawn taut with fear, her hands exploring each of the seats blindly, hopefully— but found them all empty.

'Laurent,' she called again, raising her voice. '*Où es tu?*' She started making her way towards the front of the plane, checking every space she could find.

'*Ici,*' came a hesitant whisper that she barely heard over the cacophony of sound bombarding the plane.

'*Laurent? C'est toi?*' she demanded, almost afraid to

believe what she'd heard. '*Où es tu?*' she repeated, then stayed still, her ears straining to pinpoint the little voice as soon as it came.

'*Ici*,' came the frightened whisper, and a slight movement seen out of the corner of her eye had her zeroing in on the little bundle wedged almost underneath one of the seats. '*J'ai peur . . .*' he said on a sob, his eyes enormous in his pale face.

He was frightened, Val repeated to herself, recognising the frantic tremor in the tone which matched the tremor in her own. All she had to do now was wriggle herself forward just a little bit more and. . . Ow! She yelped silently as she ducked her shoulder under the edge of one of the seats which had been wrenched up from its moorings and caught her knee on something sharp just as she reached him.

'*Laurent. Où as-tu mal?*' Val asked gently. Fear that he might be badly injured meant that she hardly dared to touch him in spite of the urge to grab him and escape this awful place as soon as possible.

'*Ma tête*,' he moaned softly, closing his eyes tightly as one grubby hand came up to hover over the side of his head. '*J'ai mal à la tête.*'

Val ran a gentle hand over the thick head of hair, dreading to find the ominous stickiness of blood, but all she came across was a tender bump above one ear which made the youngster moan again.

'*Viens, Laurent. Sortir avec moi*,' she invited, stroking his little hand with one finger and swallowing a lump in her throat when he grasped her hand with utter trust.

'*Maman?*' he queried fearfully as his wide eyes took in the destruction around him for the first time. '*Où est Maman?*'

'*Dehors*,' she reassured him as she helped him to slide out of the confined space under the seat, shielding his head with her hand to prevent him hitting it again. '*Elle t'attend*,' she promised, knowing that his mother was indeed waiting for him outside and would doubtless welcome him with open arms.

'Val?' a familiar husky voice called from outside in the unrelenting rain. 'Are you all right?'

'I've got him,' she called back, her voice breathless with effort as she manoeuvred her precious burden as quickly as possible towards the makeshift exit through the maze of sharp obstacles, the glimpse of grey light drawing her like a magnet.

'How is he?' Guy's tone of voice had sharpened at her announcement and Val paused briefly to glance down at the little white face resting against her as she half carried, half dragged him towards safety and freedom.

'He's alive,' she called back as she was forced to rest for a few seconds to gather her strength for the final effort, her throat tightening at the memory that her own precious child hadn't survived the awful crash which had robbed her of so much.

As she cradled the injured child a black bitterness began to rise up inside her at the sudden realisation that Simon would have been the same age as Laurent if only Michael hadn't. . . She cut the thought off before it could be completed and fought the blackness down.

'He's going to be fine,' she murmured as she stroked thick silky hair back from his smooth pale forehead with shaky fingers, then gathered him up in her arms to negotiate the last obstacles.

The final stages of the rescue went smoothly.

Once Val had handed Laurent into the willing hands

waiting out in the pouring rain and had been helped out
of her precarious captivity, it seemed mere minutes
before the rescue services had swung into action and
had opened up the front of the plane to release the pilot
from his own deadly prison.

The heavy grey clouds were making the daylight fade
even faster than normal for the time of the year while
she patiently watched Guy conferring with the paramedics over the care of their last two passengers.

Desperately she focused on the way the rain had
flattened his hair against his head and individual drops
glimmered in the darkness of his beard—anything to
take her mind off the nightmares she had just spent the
afternoon reliving.

Gradually she regained sufficient control so that,
when Guy finally waved the rescue services on their
way, only she knew that the shivers which were gripping
her were due to more than saturated clothing and an
increasingly keen February wind.

'Val!' Guy's voice was filled with horror as he
returned to her side. 'Didn't anyone get your coat for
you? You're freezing!' He began to shrug out of his own
wet jacket but she stayed his actions with a shaky hand.

'Don't bother,' she muttered through chattering teeth.
'I'd only have to take it off again when we get in
your car and then there would be two of us soaked to
the skin.'

'*Stupide!*' he muttered under his breath as he opened
up his jacket and pulled her against the warmth of his
body to wrap her within his encircling arms. '*Fou!*' he
added forcefully, but Val didn't know who he was calling mad and, as the delicious warmth seeped into her
from the broad strength of his chest, she didn't
really care.

'Come on, let's get you out of the rain,' he said, and Val nearly moaned at the thought of losing her place inside the warm cocoon which surrounded her.

She needn't have worried. Without releasing her, Guy managed to steer her towards his car as though they were taking part in some sort of sophisticated three-legged race, his body pressing against hers all along one side as he held her close.

'In you get,' he prompted with a hint of a chuckle in his voice, and she suddenly realised that he was holding the passenger door open for her.

'Thank you,' she managed through chattering teeth as she ducked her head under the lintel, hoping that the straggly hair plastered to her cheeks would hide the heat flooding her face. He must think her an absolute idiot for clinging to him like the survivor of a shipwreck when he was standing there holding the door open for her. . .

'The car will warm up quite quickly when I get the engine going,' he announced as he slid in from the other side and handed her a plaid travel blanket. 'Here. Wrap this around yourself in the meantime. It's not very thick and it's a bit damp and cold because it's been in the back of the car but it should help to stop the shivers.'

'Thank you,' she said again and her shaking hands fought with the folds of fabric until she'd managed to drape the blanket around her shoulders and over her knees.

Guy sat for a minute with the engine running, then turned the heater up to full strength.

'Oh, that's wonderful,' Val murmured as a blast of hot air circulated around her frozen feet and stirred the limp tendrils of hair against her face.

Gradually the warm air dried off the condensation

which had collected on the car windows and Val saw the last of the emergency vehicles leave the site of the crash, only the airport staff remaining to organise the removal of the crashed plane.

'Ready?' Guy enquired and it was then that Val realised that he'd been sitting watching her while the shivers gradually abated.

'I'm sorry... Of course... You shouldn't have waited for me...I suppose you've got to go to the hospital now?' Val babbled in her embarrassment.

'No. This time *I* just had to get them out in one piece, if possible. The staff on duty at the hospital will be taking over the rest of the job.'

'Oh.' She subsided with a sniff as a trickle of water ran down the length of her nose, and she was just about to brush it away with one hand buried in the blanket when a neatly folded white handkerchief appeared in front of her.

'Thanks,' she muttered as she shook it open and used it as a makeshift towel to blot up the excess water from her face and hair. In seconds it was saturated but at least the rain wouldn't be running down her nose any more.

'So much for our meal,' Guy commented wryly as they finally turned out onto the main road with a wave for the policeman on duty. 'I think we need to go home and have a hot shower.'

Suddenly Val's imagination was working overtime as she visualised his casual words in a literal way. In her mind's eye she saw the two of them together in the steamy confines of his shower, his arms wrapped around her in exactly the same way as they had been when he warmed her up inside his jacket, but this time they were both gloriously naked...

'Val? Are you all right?' The concern in his voice

drew her instantly to her senses and she flicked a startled glance at his intense expression as she murmured her agreement, relieved that he would have needed more than X-ray vision to have seen her X-rated thoughts.

What on earth was the matter with her? Val thought as she stood under the glorious warmth of a very efficient shower and shampooed her hair until each individual strand squeaked with cleanliness. She'd never been one for fantasising about anything and, since the loss of her husband had also meant the loss of her precious son, she especially didn't fantasise about men.

At last she turned the taps off and stepped out onto the soft pile of the bath mat to wrap herself in an enormous thick towel, winding a smaller one around her head to soak up some of the water from her hair.

In spite of the age of the house and the inclement weather outside, her room was beautifully warm as she sank wearily down on the stool in front of the dressing-table.

The vision which met her in the ornate mirror reminded her of a drowned rat, and she groaned as she contemplated the effort it would take to dry herself and get dressed to join Guy for dinner. At least, however, they would be dining alone, since Guy's grandmother had evidently already eaten and gone to bed.

The thought of food made her stomach grumble and she remembered that she and Guy had never stopped for the meal he had promised her, but. . . Her shoulders slumped with tiredness and she eyed the deep comfort of the double bed behind her.

I'll just stretch out and have a few minutes with my eyes shut, she decided as she unwound the towel from her head and gave her hair a desultory rub before dragging a comb through the worst of the tangles, grateful for the easy-care style.

It wasn't worth putting her nightdress on for the few minutes she'd be lying on the bed so she flicked back the bedspread and loosened the damp towel so that it fell at her feet just before she crawled under the covers and closed her eyes.

She hadn't had the dream for several years but even in her sleep she knew what was going to happen. It was always that way.

Something behind her driving her forward; something threatening which was forcing her to keep going, one foot after the other. . .her feet stepping into nothingness, her hands slippery with sweat and fear while she tried desperately to hold on to the rough branch, feeling all the while the gouges being torn in tender palms as she lost her battle with the force of gravity.

And then the sudden tumbling, bruising fall, down and down into darkness. . .inescapable, utter darkness.

'Val. . .?'

Once again she could hear the voices calling her. . . She knew of old that they never heard her replies—she was hidden too deep for the sound to escape, no matter how often she shouted and no matter how loud—but that didn't stop her trying. . .

'Val? What's the matter?'

The voice had always gone away before; had never come this close. Close enough to touch her; to rescue her from the terrible darkness.

'Val?' The insistent voice drew her out of the nightmare and back into the present and she opened her eyes to see the dark outline of a figure seated on the edge of the bed beside her, the solid shape silhouetted against the hallway light streaming in through her open bedroom door.

'Guy?' she croaked as she suddenly realised where she was and reached out to grasp hold of him just to be certain that he wasn't a figment of her imagination. 'What. . .what did you want?'

'You sounded as if you were having a nightmare,' he said softly. 'Just a minute while I close the door so our voices don't disturb Grand-mère. . .'

'No!' Val sat bolt upright in the bed to clutch at him as he started to stand and pulled him back down onto the bed, panic sending her pulse rate soaring instantly. 'Don't shut the light out! Don't make it dark. . .' Her throat closed up around the terrified whisper as he shifted again.

'OK,' he soothed, his hand settling over her frantic fingers to still their trembling. 'It's OK, Val. I'm just going to turn the light on beside the bed. All right?'

There was a brief click and she half closed her eyes against the sudden flood of soft, peachy light through the pleated lampshade on the bedside cabinet.

'Is it all right to shut the door now?' his husky voice queried and she nodded jerkily, her eyes following him across the room and watching him swing the solid door shut.

She saw him turn back towards her and then stop suddenly, his expression frozen on his face as he looked at her.

Puzzled, she glanced down at herself and gave a squeak of embarrassment as she realised that she was sitting up in the bed stark naked with the covers pooled in her lap.

Her hands fumbled to grab two fistfuls of the finely woven sheet and she slid partway down the bed as she dragged the covers right up to her chin, horribly conscious that her cheeks were flaming uncontrollably.

'I'll be all right now,' she mumbled and closed her eyes tightly in the fervent hope that when she next opened them he would have disappeared. Unfortunately, she could hear soft sounds which told her that he was walking towards the bed again, the thick carpet deadening his footfalls but not eliminating them.

'What was that all about?' his husky voice queried just before the mattress dipped under his weight and he captured one of her hands, untangling the sheet from her fingers before he threaded them with his own in a comforting clasp.

'It wasn't just a bad dream, was it?' he said, his voice quietly positive in the silence of the room.

Val opened her eyes warily, wishing that she could laugh the whole thing off—but one look at his face told her there was no point trying.

'It. . .I . . . Sometimes I have a nightmare. . .' she stammered, not daring to meet his eyes for fear that she would see scorn in them for her pathetic weakness.

'Often?' he prompted.

'N-not for several years.'

'Always the same one, or are they all different?'

His tone was so calm and non-threatening that Val found herself answering without thinking twice, all fear that he would judge her harshly suddenly forgotten.

'Always the same.' She sighed heavily. 'Always.'

'Do you know what makes it recur? Is there a particular trigger? A particular set of circumstances?'

'Sometimes,' she admitted softly, thinking about her overwhelming fear when she'd crawled through that jagged hole into the dark cramped confines of the crashed plane this afternoon and how hard she'd had to fight her own instincts to turn and get out as fast as she could.

'Can you tell me about it?' he demanded softly, his husky voice coaxing as his other hand came to join the first and he held her hand between the warm strength of his two palms.

Suddenly she knew that she *could* tell him, and there was a sense of relief as she found the first shaky words.

'It happened when I was small—about seven, I think.' The picture in her mind was of a solemn, skinny child with eyes too large for her face as she was handed over to her new foster-parents.

'John was about ten and he'd been there for a couple of months already and he was the boss.'

'He bullied you?'

'He bullied everybody,' she said in a small voice. In her mind she was once again the defenceless little girl who couldn't understand what had happened to her happy, secure little world; what had happened to her softly spoken mother that she had never come to collect her from the hospital after the ambulance had taken her there in the middle of the night.

It had been years before she had finally found out about the fire that had claimed the lives of both her parents and spared hers.

'There was a big tree right at the end of the garden. An oak, I think, with a big knobbly trunk that John said I had to climb or he wouldn't let me go back inside for supper.'

She remembered how tall the tree had seemed to her seven-year-old self and how far away the ground had appeared as he'd urged her higher and higher, the stick he'd held in his hand catching her ankles every time she paused.

She hadn't realised that the trunk was hollow until her feet had slipped over the lip, leaving her clinging desperately to her last handhold. . .

'He walked away,' she said, her voice still filled with a child's disbelief that anyone could be so cruel. 'He walked away and, when I couldn't hold on any longer, I slid down inside the tree.'

'Were you badly hurt?'

'I remember I was bruised and scraped from the roughness of the wood. . .' She drew in a shuddering breath but the next words emerged as little more than a whisper. 'I called and called but no one heard me. . .'

'How long were you in there?' he demanded, his voice deeper and huskier than ever. 'Didn't your foster-parents come out to call you in for supper?'

'I heard them calling at first, but he told them I'd run away. . .' She looked up at him, knowing that the remembered horror would be plainly visible on her face. 'It was dark when they found me. It had been dark for hours and I couldn't move; couldn't climb up; couldn't turn round. . .'

Her breathing grew faster and shallower at the remembered terror, her pulse beginning to pound as the remembered sensation of helplessness invaded every nerve.

'You idiot!' he exclaimed as he swept her into his arms. 'A trauma like that, which has made you so claustrophobic that you have to have a light on in your room, and yet you *still* had the courage to insist on going in after Laurent.'

His initial outburst had made Val stiffen apprehensively but when she found herself surrounded by the warmth and security of his powerful arms she relaxed gratefully, basking in the comfort of his approbation.

'I couldn't let him die,' she murmured. 'It wasn't his fault and he didn't deserve to die. He deserved to live and so did Simon. . .' The link between the two young boys filled her mind with pain and suddenly she found herself weeping helplessly, her face pressed tightly against Guy as the anguish of two years escaped her control, welling up uncontrollably and spilling over for the first time.

'How could he do it. . .?' she wailed brokenly as her shoulders shook with the force of her sobs. 'How could Michael do it to Simon. . .? He was only three years old. How could he kill our baby. . .his own son?'

CHAPTER FOUR

'WHAT?'

Even in the depths of her misery Val felt the shock hit Guy with the force of a bullet, his arms tightening around her sharply before he pushed her to arm's length.

She gazed up at him, his outline wavering through the tears which had yet to fall.

'Val.' His insistent voice was accompanied by a brief shake, his hands clutching her naked shoulders but this time oblivious to her lack of clothing. 'Did you say your husband murdered your son?' He sounded so utterly appalled that the words actually registered through the haze of her misery.

'Yes,' she whispered through quivering lips as the tears spilled over and tracked their way down her cheeks.

'Why? How?' He shook his head in disbelief. 'Didn't you do anything to stop him?'

'I didn't know,' she wailed defensively, certain that she could hear accusation in the words. 'He said he was taking Simon out to give me a r-rest and. . .and not to w-worry if they were l-late. He seemed to have forgotten it was my b-birthday but I thought he was t-teasing and they were going out to buy my p-present. . .'

She shook her head, unable to continue as sobs wracked her slender frame. Didn't he think she would have done anything in her power to keep her precious son safe? But she honestly hadn't known what Michael had intended doing when he left that day holding Simon's hand. . .

Guy released his hold on her shoulders and for a moment she felt utterly abandoned—until she was surrounded by the warm security of his arms and was cradled once again against him.

For long minutes there was only the sound of her weeping as one hand cradled her head against his shoulder and the other rubbed slow circles over her back.

Gradually she grew calmer, in spite of the fact that she knew he was going to insist that she finish telling the story.

Slowly she became aware that he must have been ready to go to bed. With her head cradled against him, she could smell that his skin was redolent of soap and freshly showered male and the wet clothing he'd cradled her against earlier in the day had been replaced by a silky robe of some sort.

'What happened?' he demanded finally. 'How could he. . .? What did he. . .? Tell me,' he finished bluntly when he couldn't find any other words.

'He crashed the car—deliberately,' she said in a thready voice, the words seeming to echo in the quiet room.

'How can you be so certain that it wasn't an accident?' he questioned carefully. 'You know as well as I do that even careful drivers can be involved in situations which make them crash.'

'On an almost clear road, with no other vehicles involved, and a witness who said that he watched Michael aim the car straight for the bridge support without attempting to brake?' Val detailed in a monotone which made it obvious that she had gone over the words again and again in her head.

She heard Guy draw in a shocked breath, felt his chest expand under her cheek and became aware of the steady thunder of his heartbeat.

'For God's sake, why?' he demanded fiercely, cradling her head in one hand and tilting it back so that he could see her face. 'Why did he do it?'

'He hadn't been well for several months. Nothing specific at first, but his moods were so changeable. One minute he didn't care what was happening and the next. . . Obstinate wasn't the word for it!' She gave a half-hearted chuckle. 'At first I thought it was something to do with the fact that he had entered his thirties—worrying about his chances for a consultancy or something—and I tried to be supportive and encouraging but. . .' She shook her head. 'It got worse.'

'Did he see anyone about it?'

'Eventually.' She sighed. 'Our GP looked him over and took a blood test but all he said was that he thought he'd probably got a touch of ''yuppie flu'' as a result of stress. I disagreed. I knew he wasn't himself and suggested that he arrange to have further tests done at the hospital.'

'Did they find anything?'

'Oh, yes. They found something, all right. It took them a long time and dozens of tests while they eliminated all the possibilities, and all the while his moods were gradually getting worse and worse—some days I almost thought he must be going mad; I know he nearly drove me to it. Finally, he told me that they'd diagnosed multiple sclerosis.'

He was silent, waiting for her to continue, somehow knowing that there was more to come.

'I was shocked at first,' she said with a slight tremor in her voice. 'The onset of the illness had been insidious enough, but for some reason I hadn't even thought of MS and had to sit down and think about the effect it would have on our lives if the disease progressed rapidly. I had to plan how we'd cope with it in the long term when he couldn't work any more...'

Her voice died away as she became lost for a moment in the events of two years ago.

'He really seemed to have accepted the diagnosis,' she continued as if there had been no pause. 'He seemed so much calmer, as if it had just been the uncertainty which had been making him so tense and angry.'

'I could understand, in a way, if he'd just decided he couldn't cope with the idea of becoming helpless,' Guy offered quietly. 'Not many men would accept that idea easily. But...why take your son with him?'

'Because it wasn't MS,' Val said flatly. 'He'd lied to me about the diagnosis. He must have known that if he'd told me what the consultant said I would have known that he'd been told not to drive, and I would have insisted that he left Simon at home if he didn't let me do the driving.'

'So, what was the matter? Schizophrenia? A brain tumour?'

'Nothing so simple,' she said wryly. 'I found out from the post mortem that he had Huntington's chorea.'

'But that's an incurable hereditary disease!' Guy exclaimed, obviously shocked. 'It can only be passed on by someone who suffers from the disease. He was a doctor, for heaven's sake. He must have *known* that—'

'He didn't know,' she interrupted. 'His parents were both dead by the time he was in his teens so he never knew that either of them suffered from it,' Val said, giving him the benefit of the long silent hours she'd agonised over the same questions.

'So neither of you knew the risks you were running when you had Simon—the fact that he had a fifty per cent chance of developing the disease any time after he turned thirty.'

She shook her head, feeling her hair catch on his beard as he rested his cheek on top of her head and they both fell silent in the quiet house.

'Had you ever thought,' he began softly as though he was thinking aloud, 'that he might have had some sort of seizure at the wheel—an attack of chorea? If the lack of control was unexpected—perhaps the first time it had happened—he might have lost control of the car before he realised it and been unable to steer it to safety. . .'

He left the words hanging, his idea unfinished for her to take or leave as she chose, and for the first time in nearly two years she felt the weight of sorrow lighten a little.

'Oh, Guy, do you really think it could have happened like that?' she pleaded as she gazed up at his face in the softly lit room. 'It's been tearing me apart to think that Michael deliberately set out to kill Simon—I was so certain that he loved him as much as I did.'

Guy tightened his arms around her in silence and eased her head back against his shoulder. She relaxed against him with a fractured sigh, revelling in his strength and warmth as she drifted slowly into a doze without the least fear that the nightmare which had woken her would return.

Val woke up to watery sunshine desperately trying to break through the heavy grey clouds which filled the section of sky she could see out of her window.

She lay warmly cocooned under the bedclothes and

was wondering idly what time it was when there was
a brief tap on the heavy wooden door.

'Come in,' she called cheerfully. It wasn't until she
began to slide herself up against the pillow to greet
whoever was opening the door that she realised that
underneath the bedclothes she was stark naked and the
memory of last night's events flooded over her.

'Good morning,' Guy's husky voice greeted her as
he pushed the door closed behind him with one foot
and carried a laden tray across the room towards her.
'Did you sleep well?' he enquired with all the aplomb
of a well-trained servant as he reached her side.

'Y-yes, thank you,' Val stammered, still trying to
come to terms with the fact that she wasn't wearing a
stitch of clothing, and the man who had held her in his
arms last night while she wept her heart out was standing in front of her with a breakfast tray in his capable
hands and a wicked grin displaying a row of gleaming
white teeth.

'If *mademoiselle* would like to sit up, I will put her
breakfast tray on her lap,' he suggested.

'No, *mademoiselle* would *not* like to sit up until she
has put some clothing on,' she muttered through
clenched   teeth   as   her   face   suffused   with
embarrassed heat.

'I can wait,' he said with a display of infinite patience.

'No, you can't,' she objected, with the bedclothes
clutched firmly under her chin. 'You can leave the tray
on the little table over by the window and I'll fetch it
when I'm ready, thank you very much.'

'Spoilsport,' he muttered with a comical leer before
he turned to do her bidding, settling the tray safely
down before he came back to her side and fixed her
with a serious gaze.

'Joking apart,' he said in a husky voice which reminded her all too clearly of his gentleness in the night, 'were you able to sleep properly after all the trauma?'

'Yes,' she said with a smile as she looked up at the concerned expression on his face. 'I don't remember falling asleep so I can't have thanked you for your kindness last night. You're a very nice man.'

'Ah! You wound me!' Guy exclaimed theatrically as he clutched his chest. 'How can you possibly condemn me to niceness when I want to be devastatingly attractive, or even irresistible—especially when I'm alone in a bedroom with a naked lady,' he added in a conspiratorial tone.

'A gentleman wouldn't have mentioned that!' she scolded with a return of heat to her cheeks.

'Ah, but who said I was a gentleman?' he retorted incorrigibly and made his way towards the door. 'It seems to me that they never seem to have as much fun as rogues do!' And he let himself out of her room with a final wink and a 'See you later'.

'Oh, you're a clever man, Guy de Bourges,' she murmured as she replayed their encounter in her mind. 'After that bit of nonsense how could I be embarrassed in your presence, in spite of telling you all my deepest, darkest fears and howling my eyes out on your shoulder last night?'

When he'd come into the room she'd hardly had time to do more than register the fact that she still wasn't wearing any clothing when he'd started teasing her and playing the fool as if he'd known that she would rather have hidden herself away than face him, knowing he'd seen her at her worst—not to mention holding her naked body in his arms as casually as if she'd been dressed for a polar expedition.

'A very clever man,' she repeated as, wrapped in her robe, she sat down to an individual pot of heavenly coffee and a plate full of warm buttery croissants wrapped in a white cloth.

'My dear! What a terrible thing to happen!' Madame de Bourges exclaimed when Val entered the small salon. 'You come here to help me and have a little holiday and what occurs? You end up having to rescue little children!'

Val made a deprecating sound, glad that her hostess had been in bed when she and Guy had returned from the airport last night soaked to the skin. She had been so disturbed by the dredging up of old memories that she didn't think she could have managed to talk about her part in the events so soon after they happened without breaking down.

She smiled briefly when she realised that the fact that she was able to make light of the events to his grandmother this morning was another thing she should thank Guy for. His calm presence and his insistence that she tell him about her childhood trauma and the terrible loss of her little son seemed, in some strange way, to have helped her to begin to come to terms with them at last.

'And have you done your exercises today?' Val interjected in the hope that she could persuade the elderly lady to change the subject, knowing that the physiotherapist wouldn't be back until Monday.

'Of course! Guy helped me before he went to the hospital, but you can help me when I do them again later. I really think I am improving now. Soon I will be able to go out without my sticks so that people don't treat me like a pathetic old lady!'

Val chuckled her appreciation. Simone de Bourges was definitely the last person you would call pathetic and, if you were counting her sheer zest for life, she was still far from old.

'I only hope that I have half of your spirit and determination when I reach your age,' she commented truthfully. 'You put the younger generation to shame!'

Her hostess preened herself a little at the compliment, then decided that she wanted to get on with her tapestry.

'Guy was quite right,' she said decisively as she began work. 'I seem to have been working on these endless flowers for ever. Now that I have seen your work, I think my next project shall be a picture—a big picture.'

'How about a copy of the Bayeux tapestry?' Val suggested, tongue-in-cheek.

Her companion chuckled. 'That would really frighten Guy!'

'Why?' Val demanded with mock innocence as she picked up the next colour for her own tapestry. 'With *your* determination, you would have it finished in a matter of weeks!'

Madame de Bourges insisted on a full account of the happenings at the hospital when her grandson finally arrived home in time for the evening meal.

'And how are all your patients from the aeroplane?' she demanded, almost before he had settled himself in his seat at the table.

'As well as can be expected.'

Val smiled when she heard the universal noncommittal phrase but it had as little effect on Madame as it

would have had on an investigative journalist, barely
slowing her down before she flung the next questions
at him.

'And the poor pilot? Are his injuries very bad?'

'Bad enough,' he said equally cryptically as he
glanced across at Val with a wry expression, inviting her
to join in his amusement at his grandmother's hunger for
specifics. 'But you know I refuse to tell you all the
gory details when we're about to eat.'

'Pah!' she exclaimed dismissively. 'Whose stomach
is so delicate that they are not interested in the condition
of their fellow man? The two of you are in the medical
profession and when your *grand-père* became ill, I did
my share of taking care of the sick.'

'Nevertheless,' Guy returned calmly, 'I would prefer
to enjoy my meal without reliving the worst parts of
my day.'

'*Ah, Guy! Il est mort?*' she deduced sorrowfully.

'No, Grand-mère, he's still alive, but he might lose
his leg. . . Oh! You do this to me every time!' he
exclaimed, his voice a mixture of humour and disgust.

'Wouldn't it be easier just to tell her what she wants
to know?' Val enquired, fighting to stop laughter erupt-
ing. She had never witnessed this sort of family give
and take before and it fascinated her.

In the whole of her nearly twenty-nine years the only
person that she could ever remember being close to was
Michael, and *their* relationship had been very different.

Perhaps it was because each of them had endured a
rather lonely childhood, or perhaps they had each been
solitary by nature. Whatever the reason, hindsight told
her that theirs had been more of a partnership than a
true meeting of hearts and minds.

Not that she had been aware of it at the time; she'd

been very happy with her marriage, in spite of the uncer-
tainties of the last few months—right up to the moment
when she'd opened the door and found the policewoman
standing on the step.

Even then, in spite of the fact that her love had turned
to hatred when she realised that Michael had killed their
precious son, she hadn't realised that there had been
anything lacking in their relationship. It was only during
the last few days that she had begun to wonder if there
might have been something missing; if there might be
something more. . .

Val's thoughts ground to a halt when she realised
where they were leading her. Why was she thinking
such things, and why were such strange ideas only
occurring to her now, two years after Michael's death?

The sound of the teasing conversation which had
been continuing between Guy and his grandmother had
faded into the background while she grappled with the
sudden avalanche of new ideas and feelings.

She felt a puzzled frown pleating her forehead as she
gazed across at Guy's handsome face as though the
answers were written there, unaware that she was
staring at him until his dark eyes met hers questioningly.

Confused and embarrassed, she dragged her eyes
back down to the plate of food she'd hardly touched
and forced herself to start eating, but she was still unable
to dredge up any more than monosyllabic replies to the
conversation going on around her.

'Is something the matter?' Guy's voice startled her as
she walked slowly back into the cosy warmth of the
small salon after she'd escorted his grandmother up to
her room.

Still plagued by the unsettling thoughts which had

assailed her earlier, she'd been totally unaware of the shadowy figure apparently waiting for her to return to the dim light of the firelit room.

'Oh!' Val gave a breathless squeak of surprise as she turned towards the voice, her hand still hovering by the light switch. 'I didn't know you were there.'

He was sitting in one of the comfortable chairs by the crackling fire, his long legs stretched out towards the hearth as he lounged back against the soft upholstery.

One hand cradled a glass of amber liquid on the arm of the chair, the firelight fragmented into gleaming shards by the decorative facets cut around the bowl.

'Would you like some Rémy Martin?' He lifted his own glass towards her. 'I only indulge when I'm not on call.'

She'd been hovering uncertainly in the doorway, drawn by the fire which, in this sensitively modernised house, was only really needed as a focal point in the room.

His invitation overcame her ambivalence about joining him and she stepped silently towards the other side of the fireplace and the matching chair she was beginning to think of as hers.

'That would be lovely,' she said with a smile. 'Just a small one—I'm not accustomed to drinking very much.'

Guy swiftly straightened up out of his chair, the movement startling her so that she took a rapid step backwards when he leant towards her, feeling strangely threatened by his silent presence in the dimly lit room—especially with his expression half hidden by his beard.

He froze, his eyes as keen as lasers as he fixed them on her face as though he wanted to read the thoughts going through her head.

Almost in slow motion he reached out to place his

glass on the mantelpiece, his eyes never leaving her for a second as he took one step towards her and pausing again when she was unable to prevent herself taking a matching pace away from him.

Suddenly aware of what she had done, Val glanced hastily at the chair just behind her and sat down in a hurry, catching her lower lip between hidden teeth in vexation as he turned sharply away from her and went across to pour her drink.

It was one thing for her to have realised that she had become frighteningly aware of Guy's presence in a room—to feel a strange electrical charge raise the tiny hairs on her skin whenever he came too close, but it was another thing entirely for her to react like a frightened virgin shying away from a potential seducer—as if Guy would need to resort to such measures to persuade a woman into accepting his attentions!

'Here,' he said gruffly, holding her glass almost at arm's length to give it to her before he returned to his own chair, one hand reaching out to retrieve his abandoned glass from the shadows of the mantelpiece.

This time when he sat down he looked anything but relaxed, his shoulders tense and his expression preoccupied as he gazed into the fire.

'Are you frightened of me?' he questioned suddenly, his eyes piercing the dimness as though he wanted to read her expression as well as hear her reply.

'What? No! Of course not,' she replied, the words coming swiftly. And as far as they went, they were the truth. The only trouble was, as she said them, she was beginning to realise that it was not Guy she feared but her growing reaction to him.

She had managed to look him in the eye when she

spoke but her thoughts could all too easily let her
expression reveal her ambiguity and she fixed them on
the deep amber-coloured liquid in her glass.

'Then why did you shy away from me?' he charged,
the muscles at the corners of his jaw clenching rhythmi-
cally as a measure of his tension. 'What did you think
I was going to do?'

'N-nothing,' Val stammered, feeling a sudden pressure behind her eyes as the situation went from bad to
worse. 'I didn't. . .I don't. . .' She subsided, shaking her
head when she couldn't find the words she wanted, then
burst out suddenly, 'I trust you!' and sat in mesmerised
horror, unable to drag her eyes away from him when
she heard her vehemence echo around the room.

As she watched Guy drew in a deep breath and, as
he released it in a steady stream, she saw the tension
leave him.

'Thank you,' he murmured huskily, his taut
expression softening with the beginnings of a smile.
'I thought that I must have done something to offend
you. . .'

Val shook her head numbly, amazed that he had been
so affected by her reaction. She was unaccustomed to
the idea that anyone could be so sensitive to her
thoughts and feelings—there had certainly never been
such a connection between Michael and herself. . .

She drew her thoughts to a screeching halt, a feeling
of guilt flooding through her.

Michael had been her husband for five years before
he was taken ill, and she owed him her loyalty. She
couldn't possibly be comparing what she had with him
against the strange sensations passing between herself
and Guy. For heaven's sake, he was little more than a
stranger. . .

'Would you like to visit the hospital tomorrow?'

Guy's husky voice broke into her frantic thoughts, the deep velvety tones stroking her nerves and sending a shiver up her spine.

For one mad moment she had to fight the urge to leap out of her chair and run away from him as far and as fast as she could but sanity prevailed, along with the decision that if she was to spend some time in his company perhaps this strange attraction would simply disappear.

'Yes,' she said, hoping that he couldn't see how fast her pulse was beating or he would never believe her calm pose. 'I'd like to have a look around—in spite of the fact I'm supposed to be on holiday!'

His teeth gleamed whitely in the firelight as he smiled. 'Well, you can put it down to comparative research and tell all your colleagues back in England how their French counterparts operate.'

'What time do you need to leave? Will there be someone here for your grandmother?'

'I'm not due in until ten tomorrow, but I would prefer to leave earlier because of our current staff shortages.'

'Oh.' Val tried to hide her disappointment. 'I'd better wait until another day, then, or she'll be alone until the physiotherapist comes.'

'Berthe will be here by eight, and then some of her contemporaries are joining her for lunch,' he offered, and her spirits rose like helium-filled balloons.

'In which case, I'll be ready to leave as soon as Berthe arrives,' she confirmed with a smile. 'We daren't risk her jeopardising her progress by giving her the chance to sneak out to go mountain-climbing or horse-racing before Berthe gets here!'

He snorted. 'You seem to have taken her measure,' he joked.

'She's a wonderful lady,' Val said with a smile. 'I really envy you having her for a grandmother.'

'Take her! You can have her!' he exclaimed as he pushed himself up out of the comfort of his chair. 'She's so strong-willed that she drives me round the bend!'

'And she couldn't possibly have passed that trait on to you, could she?' Val teased pointedly as she accepted his offered hand to help her to her feet, forgetting in the midst of the light-hearted banter that there was any reason to avoid the contact.

His lean fingers wrapped themselves firmly around her more slender hand with a silent impact that should have shed sparks.

One sustained pull brought her out of her chair with a rush so that she nearly collided with him, coming to rest with one hand braced against the thin fabric of his shirt where it lay smoothly over the breadth of his chest.

Like a doe caught in the bright beam of car headlights she froze, her eyes widening in response when she saw the awareness of their proximity hit him too.

In the flickering firelight his face was all planes and angles, the closely trimmed beard lending it an exotic air of mystery as he slowly drew her into his arms.

'Val. . .' he whispered huskily, his eyes focusing on her mouth as she nervously caught her lower lip between her teeth, then his head angled towards her and she closed her eyes in willing surrender.

CHAPTER FIVE

GUY'S lips were soft and warm as they touched hers, the contact unexpectedly tentative as though he wasn't certain how she would react to the caress.

The sharp twist of awareness deep inside her was totally unexpected, making her gasp with surprise, and he took advantage immediately. The slight roughness of his beard brushed her face as he tilted his head, his tongue gently bathing her lip where she'd bitten it before he matched his mouth to hers with a husky moan.

For a second every muscle in her body went tense at the startling sensations and then she softened, responding to the touch of his mouth on hers and his body against hers as though this was where she belonged.

His arms wrapped around her, pulling her into his lean strength until their bodies fitted together, curve against plane, softness against hardness, until she felt as if she no longer knew where she ended and he began.

'Val,' she heard him whisper, his breath warming her tender skin as she arched her neck to allow him greater access. 'Ah, *Valentine, que tu es belle,*' he groaned huskily as his hands shaped the curves of her shoulders and smoothed down her back to her waist.

It took several seconds for her to realise that she hadn't needed to translate his words from the French—her comprehension of the compliment had been instantaneous and caused a warm glow to spread through her.

It took several more seconds before she realised that

she had never reacted as quickly or as strongly as this
before—her lips had never ached and clung and her
body had never melted with nothing more than a kiss.

What she and Michael had shared had been a pale
shadow of the feelings storming through her now and
it seemed wrong. She shouldn't he reacting like this;
shouldn't be allowing his lips to taste and tantalise or
his hands the liberty to roam.

'Guy,' she murmured, forcing herself to turn her head
away as she tried to escape the arousing temptation of
his lips. 'Guy. . .I can't. . . We can't do this. . .' she
began as guilt began to gnaw at her conscience.

'Can't do what?' Each word was a caress as he whispered distractedly, and her heavy lids lifted just far
enough to glimpse the dark fans of his absurdly long
lashes spread across the fire-lit flush of his cheek-bones
before he captured her mouth again, his tongue teasing
and tantalising her until, briefly, her eyes closed and she
allowed him access to the deep recesses of her mouth.

'No!' she cried in a strangled voice when she finally
surfaced far enough to wrench herself out of his arms.
'We *can't* do this. It's not right.'

Every cell in her body was thrumming with an electrical charge as she stood there quivering with shameful
arousal and suffered his fierce scrutiny.

'How can it be wrong?' he demanded, for the first
time his accent sounding 'foreign' to her ears. 'Neither
of us is married and we are attracted to each other. . .'
He reached out to trail one finger along her cheek.

She shivered with instant awareness and turned her
face away to break the tenuous contact, the guilt growing stronger.

'But we don't know each other,' she objected
fiercely, angry with herself that this situation had arisen

in the first place. 'We met just a few days ago. . .'

'Ah!' he broke in as though he suddenly understood what she meant. 'The English have a timetable for these things, do they?'

'Yes. . . No. . .!' She shook her head, thoroughly rattled, and ignored his facetious remark. 'I'm not ready for. . . It's too soon. . . Anyway, I'm already. . .' She stumbled to a halt, horrified by the words she'd nearly said.

I'm already married.

They echoed hollowly in her mind as though she'd actually said them and she felt as if she were being torn asunder.

She'd actually used them as an excuse once, about three months ago, when a new SHO had joined the staff and wouldn't accept a simple refusal and they'd felt valid. In some strange way she'd still felt as if she *was* married to Michael.

Not this time, though.

Something inside her had rebelled against using Michael as a shield, even though Guy had wanted far more than her company for a simple date.

Some of her shock and confusion must have shown on her face because suddenly his expression softened and he gave a quintessentially Gallic shrug.

'All right, Val,' he said gently, raising both hands in a gesture of surrender. 'I will respect your wishes but, in return, you will spend some of your time with me so that we can get to know each other, as you suggested.'

'But I didn't say. . .'

'I have some paperwork I should look through before I go to bed tonight,' he continued as though she hadn't spoken. 'I'll say goodnight, and see you in the morning as arranged.'

His final words drifted back to her over his shoulder as he turned and left the room, for all the world as though the last quarter of an hour had been spent in nothing more than innocuous conversation.

'Wretched man!' Val muttered for the umpteenth time in the last few hours as she turned over and thumped her pillow viciously. 'How am I supposed to be able to sleep when I can't switch my brain off?'

It was true that she'd been lying there trying to sort out her muddled thoughts but, if she was honest, it was her feelings which were keeping her awake.

Guy's suggestion that Michael might have been just as much a victim of the car crash as Simon had removed some of the terrible burden of anger against him that she'd been carrying about with her for the last two years.

But, instead of her relief resurrecting her love for him and making Michael's memory grow dearer to her, it actually seemed to be permitting her to step away from him, as though the resolution of that anger was letting her finally put him to rest. . .

Slow tears seeped out in spite of her tightly closed lids and she gave in to the expression of sadness at the loss of her husband.

Before her sorrow had always been tempered by her anger that he'd apparently taken the decision to spare himself and his son the horrendous future which awaited sufferers of Huntington's chorea without consideration for *her* feelings.

Ultimately she'd had to acknowledge that if he'd decided that he couldn't face a future in which his body and mind would deteriorate into chaos and dementia, it was his choice. Her grief and anguish had been centred on the fact that he'd also made the decision arbitrarily

for their precious son and had wiped out both their lives
without allowing her the chance to say goodbye. . .

'God, that sounds so selfish,' she murmured into the
light afforded by the soft peach bedside lamp. 'He
would have known that I would try to stop him. . .' And
she would have. She'd have fought tooth and nail. . .

She sighed deeply as her thoughts ranged over such
familiar ground, then paused when she realised that this
time it was different.

This time the fierce anger and resentment she'd
always felt towards him that he hadn't given her the
chance to talk about his options had faded until her
predominant emotion was one of sadness—sadness for
the waste of the two lives lost in that fatal crash, no
matter how the crash had happened.

But it wasn't sorrow for the loss of her husband and
son which crept over her as she finally managed to drift
off to sleep in the early hours of the morning. Her last
thoughts were of the sweet gentleness of Guy's lips as
they'd claimed hers in the fire-lit darkness of the salon
and the fierce strength and heat of his body when he'd
held her tightly in his arms.

'*Bonjour.*'

Guy's husky voice greeted Val as she entered the
little breakfast room. He looked across at her, his dark
eyes skimming over her from head to foot and leaving
her tingling as though a bolt of lightning had passed
close by before they dropped back to the table.

Val had to clench her fists inside the pockets of her
long-line waistcoat to control the surge of pleasure that
had ripped through her as soon as she saw him, closely
followed by a pang of hurt that he seemed to have
dismissed her presence so quickly.

'Good morning,' she returned quietly, hoping he would believe the pose of calmness she was hanging on to by a thread.

How dared he look so handsome and well-rested when she'd tossed and turned for half the night? She'd had to resort to wearing twice her normal amount of make-up to hide the ravages of a poor night's sleep. Was she the only one who had been affected by their passionate kisses and subsequent disagreement?

As she pulled out a chair and sat down on the other side of the table he hooked one lean finger under his gleaming white shirt cuff to glance at his watch, then folded the newspaper he'd been reading.

'I'll be ready to go in about ten minutes,' he announced as he straightened up from his own seat and left the room without another word.

'Ten minutes it is,' she muttered as she helped herself to a warm, buttery croissant from the small basketful on the table, broke it open to receive a layer of apricot conserve, then reached for the coffee-pot to pour herself a large cup of the fragrant brew. 'I've a feeling I'm going to need this,' she said aloud as she raised it to her lips for the first delicious sip.

The terrible weather seemed to have eased a little, the grey sky several shades lighter than the last time she'd seen it, but the tributaries to the river Vilaine that they passed on their way into Rennes itself were very full of water, and it looked as if it wouldn't take much more rain for the whole system to burst its banks.

'Is there much danger of flooding around here?' Val asked finally, when it seemed as if their whole journey was to pass in silence.

'We get a fair amount of rain—that's why the area

is so lush and green——but this has been an exceptionally wet winter.'

'And looks like being an equally wet spring,' she added pointedly. 'I'm glad it's not just England that suffers from this sort of dismal day.'

'England just suffers from more of them,' he gibed. 'Or, at least, that's what everyone would have us believe!'

Val heard the thaw begin in his voice as he took advantage of the chance to taunt her, and she smiled secretly at the fact that it was a discussion about the great British standby topic of conversation which had brought about the change.

'It's probably just because we talk about it more,' she suggested, and breathed a sigh of relief. It had been well worth the effort of breaking the silence, otherwise the rest of her stay in his home would have been very uncomfortable. At least now they were more or less on speaking terms.

'Will you be able to find out how the victims of the plane crash are doing?' Val requested as she followed Guy towards the hospital entrance, no longer surprised by his courtesy when he automatically held the door open and gestured for her to precede him into the warmth.

'I'll do it as soon as I find out what horrors are waiting for me now. Perhaps we can pay them a visit as soon as I've got a minute free.'

Val nodded her agreement, then found herself fighting to remember the French she'd learned when he embarked on a fast round of introductions.

'Help!' she yelped when another couple of nurses approached, drawn by the group surrounding the two of them. 'I'll never remember everyone's names and

I've never learnt the words for "Hey! You!" in French.'

'There are actually far fewer staff on duty than usual,' Guy told her as he led her through the department and pointed out the various speciality areas. 'There's been a flu epidemic coinciding with a pregnancy epidemic, and neither one has run their course yet.'

Val chuckled at the thought of a pregnancy epidemic but had to concede, as they completed their tour, that there did seem to be an unusually large number of suspiciously rotund women on the staff.

'A couple of the administrators have volunteered to come back in to help cover for sick colleagues, in spite of the fact that they're officially on maternity leave,' he explained when she pointed out one woman who looked at least ten months' pregnant.

'I suppose they're in as safe a place as possible if the babies decide to arrive while they're at work,' she pointed out in the hearing of one such lady.

'Well,' she responded with a cheeky sideways glance at Guy, 'if this flu epidemic gets much worse it will depend just how busy the department is when I actually start my labour whether they'll make me finish my shift first!'

'Monique! You'll be giving Val a terrible impression of us!' Guy protested, but the two women shared a knowing smile before he led her through to the staff-room where she could have a cup of coffee while she waited for him to take a break.

The morning passed surprisingly quickly. At first the various members of staff chatted pleasantly in a mixture of French and English when they found her there, but it wasn't long before she found herself following them back out into the department to continue a conversation when their break was over.

It was a very short step from there to lending a help-ing hand when an injured woman came in with two terrified youngsters clinging to her.

Val could see that they were far too frightened to let go of her, their fear of their strange surroundings only surpassed by their horror at their mother's profusely bleeding injury.

Unfortunately this meant that until they could be dis-tracted noone could get close enough to take care of her.

'*Je m'appelle Valentine et je suis anglaise,*' she said, crouching down to their level and putting on a comical parody of an English/French accent to introduce herself. '*Comment vous appelez-vous?*'

The silence in the room was suddenly deafening, as if no one could believe what they were hearing—least of all the two children who peered wide-eyed at her from behind their mother.

'Pierre,' one hazel-eyed imp volunteered nervously, without letting go of his tight hold on his mother's jacket. '*Je m'appelle Pierre.*'

'Philippe,' his identical little brother added, peering out shyly from behind her.

'Twins!' Val exclaimed in delight. '*Les jumeaux!*' she translated when they looked at her in confusion.

In no time at all she was making them laugh by demanding that they teach her the French words for the various parts of their bodies, and pretending to mispro-nounce each one. They quickly became engrossed in correcting her attempts and their tight grip on their mother began to ease while they insisted that Val prac-tise her vocabulary until she did it to their satisfaction.

In the meantime the nursing staff were able to approach close enough to make an examination of the wound and they were soon free to take care of Madame Giraud, unhindered by two clinging children.

Guy had arrived partway through Val's pantomime to stitch the nasty wound on their mother's head, and she overheard the poor woman's description of how her foot had slipped off the wet edge of the pavement as she was about to load her shopping in the car and had overbalanced and struck her head hard on the edge of the car door.

Meanwhile the twins had lost all their shyness and were subjecting Val to a grilling.

'*D'où êtes vous?*' demanded Pierre.

'*L'Angleterre.*'

'*Que faites-vous?*' Philippe chimed in.

'*Je suis infirmière,*' she replied, then smiled at their scepticism when they pointed out that she wasn't dressed the same as the other nurses. '*Je suis ici en vacances,*' she explained, but they were already off on another topic.

'*Est-ce que le médecin est votre mari?*' Pierre demanded, pointing towards Guy as he bent over their mother.

Val's eyes flew towards him, hoping that he hadn't heard the children's speculation about their relationship, but he must have been listening because at that moment he glanced towards Val with a wicked expression in his eyes and she felt the sudden surge of heat which told her that she was blushing.

'No—er—*non*,' she stammered, unable to look away from him. '*Il est mon ami*,' she managed at last, wishing she could thump him when he grinned broadly enough for all the staff in the room to put their own speculative interpretation on her innocuous words.

The one thing they couldn't know was the sudden

strange feeling of loss that had sped through Val when she realised that not only was Guy not her husband but, in spite of their heated kiss last night, he was hardly even a friend. . .

At last Madame Giraud had a dressing taped in position over the neat row of stitches Guy had used to close the wound.

After he directed one of the nurses to make sure that she received a copy of the leaflet about precautions with head injuries, he reassured her that he'd trimmed as little of her hair as possible and that, once it had time to fade, the scar would hardly show unless she went bald or took to shaving her head.

'You were enjoying yourself, weren't you?' he commented when he was finally free to escort her up to the wards where the victims of the plane crash were recovering.

'They were lovely boys,' she agreed blandly in an attempt at controlling the direction of the conversation, knowing instinctively that he was looking for a way to tease her about her reaction to the twins' questions. 'Do you know how Laurent is doing?'

'I haven't had time to check up on any of them yet today, so we'll both find out together.' He pushed open one side of the swing doors to the surgical ward and ushered her through to greet the senior nurse.

It didn't take long to find out that the young lad who had reminded her so much of Simon had recovered well and would be able to go home as soon as his mother was ready for release. As for the rest, apart from the plaster casts on broken bones and the sets of stitches which had been needed by various members of the group, the only one who was causing concern was the pilot.

'It doesn't look as though we're going to be able to save his leg,' Guy told her with a grimace after a rapid conversation too full of technical terms for Val to follow.

'It looks as if there was too much damage to the nerves and the blood supply,' he elaborated. 'And, obviously, we daren't take too many chances because he isn't in a fit state to risk the possibility of gangrene.'

'Has anyone been in to visit him?' Val asked impulsively, her heart going out to the poor man. 'Is he in a fit state for visitors?'

'Just a minute while I find out.'

She watched while he went across to the nurses' station to make his enquiries, then went to join him when he beckoned.

'Apparently he had been asking to see you,' Guy relayed as he led the way towards ICU.

'Me?' Val was startled. 'Why? I didn't have anything to do with his rescue.'

'No. But you did find his son and bring him out,' Guy said quietly as they approached the bed.

'*Monsieur. . .?*' Guy said as he leant towards the grey-faced figure on the bed, clearly not wanting to disturb him if he was getting some much-needed sleep.

'*Oui. . .*' came a hoarse whisper, and Val watched as he tried to open his eyes.

In a few words Guy told him that he had a visitor and explained who Val was.

This time his attempt was successful and Val saw his eyes were the same dark brown as his little son's.

'*Merci,*' he whispered, reaching painfully for her hand and grasping it in a surprisingly strong grip. '*Merci infiniment pour la vie de mon fils.*'

The heartfelt emotion in his voice brought tears to

Val's eyes and her throat closed up so that she wasn't able to do anything more than squeeze his hand in return.

She knew only too well the nightmares which would haunt the poor man in the days and months to come when he thought about how close he had come to losing his son.

His eyes closed and his grip weakened so that Val could slip her hand away, and she managed to grit her teeth and control the urge to cry until she'd left his bedside.

He'd thanked her for saving the life of his son and she was glad that she'd been in the right place at the right time to help. It was her own private sadness that no one had been able to save Simon's life. . .

'Are you crying?' Guy demanded in a hushed voice, ducking his head to peer at her face when they reached the comparative privacy of the long corridor.

Val shook her head silently, her teeth clenched in the soft flesh of her lower lip as she fought for control.

'I would never have brought you to see him if I'd known it would affect you like this,' he muttered as he curved one arm around her shoulders.

The warm weight felt so protective and Val suddenly realised how long it had been since there had been someone there for her—someone who cared enough about her feelings to want to console her.

Guy had comforted her when she'd woken up from her nightmare and had held her in his arms when, after two years of misery, she had finally allowed herself to cry her heart out over the loss of her husband and child.

Now, believing that their visit to the injured pilot had upset her, he was offering himself as a comforter all over again.

It was so tempting—the thought of allowing him to hold her and keep her safe from the heartbreak of life— but she knew only too well that her time in his company was limited and she didn't dare relax her guard any further; she couldn't allow herself to start to depend on him to be there for her because, once she returned to England, it would be so much harder to fend for herself again.

'I'll be all right,' she whispered and drew in a steadying breath before she straightened her shoulders. 'How long will it be before you know about his leg?' she asked, fixing her attention on the first thing that came to mind rather than dwell on the hollow ache which had invaded her at the thought of leaving France—leaving Guy.

'It depends on the circulation in his leg. He had some major damage to the blood vessels and the surgeon had to graft some sections from the other leg.'

'So if the grafts take well. . .'

'And if there aren't any other areas of damage that break down in the meantime, and if he doesn't have any problems with clotting. . .' Guy recited.

'So, although he's been rescued and come through the surgery, it's still a case of keeping our fingers crossed, is it?'

'Isn't it always?' he said wryly. 'You know as well as I do that some patients seem to be well on the way to recovery and suffer a fatal setback, while others look as if they have no chance of survival and their progress is nothing short of miraculous.'

It was time for Guy to return to his own department and Val accompanied him towards the stairwell that would lead them to the back entrance of the unit, glad that they wouldn't be sharing a lift with other staff and visitors. This way they had the chance to talk together for a few more minutes.

'It still gives me the shivers,' she murmured under her breath while she glanced out of the tall windows beside them and saw that the sky hadn't cleared any further.

'What does?' his husky voice demanded and she realised that she had spoken her thoughts aloud.

'The thought that it was almost by chance that Laurent was missed in time,' she elaborated. 'The rescue services thought they'd got everyone else out and were just about to chop the plane up to release the pilot.' She drew in a shaky breath before she could continue her thoughts, her stricken eyes meeting his. 'The jaws of that machine could have taken his little legs off.' She shuddered expressively.

'If you keep thinking like that you'll be having nightmares again,' he warned, catching her hand and giving it a squeeze. 'Not that I would mind comforting you again!' he volunteered with an air of innocence which he then spoiled by grinning wickedly, his dark eyes gleaming at her between his impossibly long lashes.

Val's heart gave a lurch as his powerful attraction hit her all over again. It wasn't fair that one man should have it all—looks, charisma, sense of humour, intelligence. . .

He seemed to have all the attributes that the men who contributed to lonely hearts magazines claimed, only in his case it was all true.

'What do you want to do while I get back to work?' he asked when they entered his domain. 'Do you want to phone for a taxi and do some more research in Rennes itself, or would you rather go back home?'

Val thought for a moment.

She hadn't brought her precious folder with her so there was no real point in trying to get any further with that project and, while Guy's reference to 'going home' sounded wonderfully welcoming, she found herself strangely reluctant to leave him.

Since she'd made the effort to break through his strange reserve during their car journey, she'd been thoroughly enjoying his company and was loath to cut short their time together.

'Would the hospital powers that be object if I hung around?' she suggested hesitantly. 'You know that I'm fully qualified and you did say that you're short-staffed at the moment. . .'

'Are you sure that's what you want to do?' He frowned. 'This is supposed to be a holiday for you, in spite of the fact that I coerced you into helping with Grand-mère.'

'I'm happier when I'm busy,' she admitted honestly.

'You don't know what you'd be letting yourself in for but, if you're sure, I could find out if there is actually anything in the rules to cover—'

He never finished the sentence as his name was called urgently by someone at the other side of the unit.

Val stayed where she was and watched the rapid conversation which took place when Guy and the heavily pregnant Monique met in the middle of the department.

She watched, fascinated, as he alternately smiled and frowned, finally grasping Monique's hands in his and leaning forward over her fully expanded waistline to kiss her cheek.

Val hardly had time to register the swift stab of envy when he turned towards her and beckoned her over to join the two of them.

'Val, two more nurses have rung in to say that they've gone down with flu and Monique will be on her way up to the maternity department in just a moment so, if you were only being polite when you offered to help out, now is the time to run away!'

Val laughed in response to his slightly frazzled look, but Monique just had time for a strangled moan as she was gripped by the beginnings of her next contraction.

'Where are the wheelchairs kept, Monqiue?' Val demanded as she automatically snapped into action. 'You should be on your way or you'll end up producing that baby down here. Guy might just be desperate enough by then to make you get right up and finish your shift!'

Guy supported Monique quietly while she concentrated on her breathing and by the time the contraction was easing Val was ready with a wheelchair and a porter to push it.

'Good luck,' she said with a smile as the young woman was wheeled away towards the bank of lifts, then turned to hand Guy the slip of paper Monique had given her at the last second. 'I'll leave it to you to tell her husband what's happening,' she suggested. 'I'm not quite confident enough of my French to pass on that sort of information on the telephone!'

'Coward!' he taunted softly in English, then beckoned one of the nurses over and switched to speaking French. 'Val is going to help out in the department today, Jacqui. Can you find her a spare uniform and put her to work? I'll make certain the hospital authorities know what's going on and have a word with your superior.'

Val was somewhat nervous of the combination of a strange hospital and a foreign language but she soon found out that sick and injured patients were the same mix of personalities, whatever their nationality.

'Hey, this is good!' Jacqui commented when Val had been working with the team for a couple of hours. 'The word's got around the patients that we've got an English nurse in the department and lots of them are asking to see you.'

'I'd noticed that most of them were wanting to practise their English conversation on me,' Val said with a smile.

'Well, as far as the rest of the staff are concerned, they can *all* chat to you,' one of the other girls chimed in. 'It means the rest of us are having an easy time of it. Even some of our "regular" customers have been on their best behaviour so that they can see you!'

'You make me sound like the newest exhibit in a zoo!' Val laughed. 'Are they expecting me to perform clever tricks?'

'You are,' confirmed Guy's husky voice as he joined the group. 'You actually persuaded those American tourists to sit down quietly and wait their turn. That's almost the same as performing miracles!'

'I think it was because they were so grateful that they'd found someone who nearly spoke the same language,' Val said wryly, and there was a round of laughter.

'Anyway—' Guy glanced down at his watch '—if you can bear to drag yourself away from this lot it's time to go home.'

Val said her cheerful goodbyes, having thoroughly enjoyed working with the friendly group, but inwardly her whole being was focused once again on the way Guy had naturally spoken about the two of them going home.

Did he have any idea how precious that phrase was

to her? It was almost exactly two years since she'd felt as if she belonged anywhere, and with just those few words he had managed to thaw something deep inside her that she'd thought would be frozen for ever.

CHAPTER SIX

'But Guy, you are so naughty, making Val work on her holiday,' Simone de Bourges remonstrated over dinner that night. 'Just because *you* must be working all the time is no excuse for dragging the poor girl—'

'Grand-mère—' be began.

'It's all right, *madame*,' Val broke in. 'I offered to help out when I saw how short of staff they were. I'd rather keep busy, even on holiday.'

'*Vraiment?*' the elderly lady demanded suspiciously.

'Yes. Really,' Val confirmed with a laugh. 'I enjoy my work.'

'And she's very good at it, too,' Guy said approvingly.

'I know that, myself, from my time in your hospital,' Madame agreed. 'I was very frightened and confused after the accident, and you were very kind.'

'And she works hard,' he added, compounding her embarrassment at such an open testimonial with the warm glow which spread through her at his approval. 'When the patients found out we had an English nurse with us they all wanted to be seen by her.'

'Well, if she's been working so hard for you, then you should thank her by taking her out for a meal,' his grandmother announced decisively.

'Oh, but. . .' Val began, torn between trying to let Guy off the hook his grandmother had placed him on and her pleasure at the idea of finally going out for a meal with him.

97

'That sounds like a good idea,' he agreed evenly. 'I won't be able to make it for a couple of days—until my next evening when I'm not on call—but I shall arrange something. Is that all right with you?'

He turned to face Val for the first time since he'd begun speaking and it wasn't until she met his narrowed gaze that she realised that his calm words in no way mirrored his feelings.

Was he angry that he had been manoeuvred into taking her out or. . .?

Her scurrying thoughts stumbled to a halt when he smiled at her and she was seared by the sudden heat of his intent expression.

She shivered, every hair going up on the back of her neck as though she had just looked into the eyes of a predator. Suddenly she had been given a glimpse of his hidden depths.

Outwardly Guy de Bourges was a civilised man all right, with his silk shirts and impeccably tailored suits, but, whether he had realised it or not, she had just seen a hint of the steely determination hidden under the sophistication and she realised that he possessed all the finely honed instincts of a ruthless hunter.

This time, she had the prickly feeling that *she* was his chosen prey but her instinctive fear was almost buried by a deep twist of excitement.

As she watched his expression changed subtly, the intensity of his gaze becoming hotter and more slumbrous, and she suddenly understood what it would feel like to be the chosen mate of a powerful wild animal.

There was a strange threatening ambivalence in knowing that you could simultaneously be the prey and the beneficiary of an undeniable force of nature.

'How about Friday?' he suggested. His expression

was smooth and calm again but the touch of gravel she could hear in his usually husky voice made her realise that he was as much a victim of the atmosphere growing between them as she was.

'Friday would be perfect!' agreed his grandmother before Val could utter a word. 'I shall ask Berthe to organise a special meal and stay here overnight, and I shall invite some of my friends to join me. Then you won't be worried that you must come home early to keep an eye on your old *grand-mère*.'

Val's eyes flew from one to the other in amazement at how the decision had been taken out of her hands, then caught sight of the suspicious movement at the corner of Guy's mouth.

'You might be wearing a beard but I can still tell when you're laughing,' she accused, and couldn't help laughing herself when he gave that 'who, me?' open-handed Gallic shrug with eyes that had lost the look of heated danger and were suddenly full of wicked innocence.

There was nothing for it but to acquiesce. Even if she hadn't wanted to go out with him she didn't think she would have been able to hold out against both of them. His grandmother, in particular, seemed determined that the two of them would go out together on Friday, her expression one of gleeful delight at the idea.

Unsettled by her tangled thoughts, it was hardly surprising that Val couldn't concentrate on her tapestry that evening.

For one thing Guy's grandmother kept up an almost constant stream of chatter as she plied her own needle, most of it about the history of the de Bourges family and—more often than not—reminiscences of Guy's childhood.

It was a good thing that after the first half-hour the man in question had taken himself off to his office at the other end of the ground floor or she wouldn't have had any peace—it was bad enough that his name was mentioned with every other sentence.

It wasn't until she finally shut her bedroom door behind her that Val allowed herself to think about the expression in Guy's eyes when he'd looked at her at the table this evening.

She'd known, the way every woman did, that he was attracted to her, even at their first brief meeting in the corridor outside his mother's room. And, after their kiss in the firelight, she'd thought that she'd understood the depths of that attraction, but the blazing ferocity of the heat in his eyes at the table this evening had shaken her to the depths of her soul.

She had never witnessed desire like it and had certainly never had it directed towards her, even in the early days of her marriage to Michael

A deliciously lazy bath had done little to take her mind off the thought of Guy's attraction towards her and, with her skin sensitised by the warm water and the moisturising lotion she'd smoothed on before slipping her nightdress over her head, she felt as if every nerve was alert—almost as if she was expecting something to happen.

She had just turned out the main light, leaving the room bathed in the soft peachy glow of the bedside lamp, and was undoing her robe before sliding under the covers when there was a soft tap at the door.

'Val?' Guy's husky voice called, low enough not to disturb her if she was already asleep.

She froze, every nerve and sinew tense as her pulse instantly began to pound heavily at the base of her throat. What was he doing at her door at this time of night? Was this what she had been waiting for?

She had a swift mental image of the intent expression on his face earlier that evening and her heart gave an extra beat of excitement which she quickly squashed.

She had seen the expression in his eyes; had felt the tension tighten between them like a fine-drawn wire, and she knew that if Guy had come to her room with seduction in mind he would hardly be standing out in the corridor knocking politely.

Another thought occurred and she grabbed the edges of her silky robe, wrapped it around herself and tied the sash swiftly around her waist as she crossed the carpet on bare feet.

She wrenched the dark wooden door open just as Guy began to turn away, his white shirt gleaming dully in the subdued light of the corridor.

'Is something wrong with your grandmother?' she demanded breathlessly. 'She hasn't been taken ill, has she?'

'What?' He seemed startled. 'No, no. She's fine. I'm sorry. . . I didn't mean to worry you like that.'

'Thank goodness,' Val said and gave way to a sigh of relief. 'I would hate for something to go wrong for her now.'

'You really like her, don't you?' he smiled. 'I've a feeling you're two of a kind in spite of the difference in your ages.'

'Thank you for the compliment,' she smiled shyly, knowing how much he respected the indomitable old lady. 'But, if it wasn't your grandmother, what did you want me for?'

There was a brief silence which suddenly prickled with awareness as his eyes dropped swiftly down the curves of her skimpily clad body and then burned hotly into hers.

Startled to feel her breasts begin to tingle and her nipples tighten with the beginnings of arousal, Val wrapped her arms around herself, drawing the edges of her burgundy-coloured silk robe closer together as though to hide her reaction from his eyes.

'I. . .' Guy paused to clear his throat before he drew in a deep breath and continued. 'I rang the hospital a few minutes ago. The flu situation is no better, so if you're willing to accompany me again tomorrow. . .'

It took several seconds before his words made sense and then Val wasn't sure whether she was disappointed that he had only come to invite her to another day's work at the hospital, or relieved that he hadn't come to. . .

'Ah. . .yes. I'd like that—provided it doesn't mean your grandmother being left alone. . .'

'I shouldn't worry about her if I were you,' he said wryly. 'She's been phoning all her friends now she's back on her feet again and the house will probably be full of a constant stream of visitors from now until she's out and about again.'

'In that case, I'd love to,' Val said enthusiastically. 'I thoroughly enjoyed myself yesterday and all that practice seems to be doing my French no end of good— in spite of the teasing over my accent.'

'That's a regional thing,' Guy said with a chuckle. 'Your accent is almost "Touraine" and, for the people here, it's noticeably different.'

'Like the difference between an Oxford accent and a West Country one, for example?'

'Almost. But as it's all French it's not really a problem.'

She suddenly shivered and realised just how long the two of them had been standing in the open doorway of her room.

'I'm sorry, Val,' Guy said penitently, laying one warm hand on the cool skin of her forearm, 'I've kept you talking so long that you're getting cold. I'll see you in the morning—at seven-thirty?'

'Seven-thirty it is,' she agreed, covering the tingling patch where he'd touched her with her own hand as she stifled a pang at the end of their impromptu conversation. She had taken a step back and was reaching for the doorhandle when Guy spoke again.

'Val?' he murmured huskily, and she swung her head towards him to find that he'd matched her small step with a stride of his own and was now standing so close to her that she had to look up to meet his eyes.

'Sleep well,' he said softly, his eyes travelling over her face as he raised one hand to trace the curve of her jaw until he reached the point of her chin.

Wordlessly he raised his eyebrows in a question, his fingertips exerting a gentle pressure to tilt her face up towards his lowering mouth.

Val stopped breathing and she could feel her eyes widening as she gazed up at the taut planes and intent eyes of his handsome face.

'Please?' he whispered, the word little more than a puff of air through lips enticingly framed by the silky darkness of his beard as he paused so that their mouths were tantalising millimetres apart.

Helplessly she allowed her eyes to close and parted her lips for him, her head dropping back submissively into the security of his cradling palm.

In an instant warmth flooded her being, inside and out, as he pulled her thinly clad slenderness against the warmth of his muscular body, surrounding her within the security of his arms and searing her with the fervour of his kiss.

She felt the deep rumble of his groan as she met the sword-thrust of his tongue with the flickering rapier of her own, delighting in their mutual duel of exploration until, finally, he gripped her shoulders in his palms and put her away from him.

'I didn't intend that to happen,' he confessed hoarsely, his breathing equally as laboured as hers as he shook his head. 'I was just going to give you a simple goodnight kiss.'

'Perhaps that's the problem,' Val murmured shakily as she began to regain the use of her legs and stopped leaning weakly against him. 'Perhaps there's no such thing as a simple goodnight kiss. . .'

'You might be right,' he admitted, taking the step which would break the contact between them and then the next one which took him out into the corridor. 'Seven-thirty,' he reiterated.

'Seven-thirty,' she repeated like a mantra as she closed the door on his retreating back.

'*Now* try to go to sleep!' she muttered despairingly as she flung herself into the bed and pulled the covers right up under her chin.

One finger came up to trace the line of her mouth wonderingly, the warmth of Guy's lips seeming to linger there, and her face still tingled from the contact with his neatly trimmed beard. She snatched her hand away and thrust it under the covers, out of the way of temptation. What on earth was the matter with her, mooning over a kiss?

Hadn't she sworn two years ago that she was going to keep a firm hold on her common sense whenever a man came too close? She'd suffered the worst losses any woman could be asked to bear—the loss of her husband and her child. Did she want to go through all that pain again?

Unfortunately, when she'd made her vow, she hadn't known that she was going to meet anyone as devastating to her senses as Guy de Bourges. All he had to do was walk into a room and she was aware of him in a way that had never happened before, but what did it mean?

Was it just a signal that she was finally recovering from her sadness and would eventually be ready to accept the companionship of a member of the other half of the human race? Or was it something far simpler— something as basic as her first taste of lust?

She groaned and rolled over to bury her face in the pillow.

She had promised to help out at the hospital and, if she was going to wake up in time, she needed to go to sleep—now!

In spite of her determination it was still some time before she finally began to drift off, and the only consolation she had was the thought that Guy had seemed to be just as affected by their kiss as she had so, if there was any justice in the world, he would be having just as much trouble falling asleep as she was.

'Sister! Quickly!'

Val now understood the French words she heard automatically, without needing to translate them. It was her third day helping at the hospital and they were still in the throes of one of the worst flu epidemics the region had suffered for years, with patients arriving almost every hour.

It didn't take long for her to look the latest victim over and call Guy to check her findings.

'She's very dehydrated, isn't she?' Val commented when he gently examined the elderly lady who had been brought in by her almost equally frail husband. 'He said she's been like this for three days.'

'He doesn't look much better,' Guy muttered in an aside.

'He's probably been ignoring his own symptoms because he's been so worried about taking care of his wife,' she replied with a lump in her throat. 'What would hospital policy be about putting up a drip for each of them?'

Guy chuckled wryly. 'I don't think one more is going to make much difference at this stage. They'll probably have to put them in hammocks slung from the rafters as it is.'

Val had been hearing about the emergency measures the hospital had been forced to adopt, with all non-essential operations postponed indefinitely both to free up the beds for emergency admissions and to help prevent passing the infection on to otherwise healthy individuals.

So far it wasn't having much effect on the availability of beds because all the hospitals in the surrounding areas were in much the same position.

Today they'd reached the stage where almost every bed was filled and the staff who were still on their feet were almost being rushed off them.

'All I can say is I'm glad I had my flu jab this year,' Val commented as she straightened up and massaged the sore muscles in the small of her back. She'd had to do so much lifting in the last three days as the patients arrived in a seriously weakened state that she'd be glad when this shift ended—and it was only mid-morning as yet.

'The whole problem isn't helped by the terrible weather,' Jacqui added. 'Some low-lying areas are already waterlogged and the forecast said there's more on the way.'

'Does that mean we'll get more people coming here if they have to be evacuated?' Val enquired, knowing she might need the information before the day was over.

'Only the injured and the sick. The rest will be taken care of in schools and churches if they don't have family and friends to take them in.'

Val mentally pictured the position of Guy's home and breathed a sigh of relief that it had been built in a relatively elevated position. It might be surrounded by flooded fields and some of the roads might become impassable, but she was reasonably certain that the house itself would withstand anything the weather could throw at it and still be standing high and dry.

Jacqui's prediction came true just before midday when Guy announced that a phone call had just come through to warn them that several villages in one of the lower-lying areas were being evacuated.

'So far there are no reports of any injuries but we'll be kept informed,' Guy said calmly. 'In the meantime we'll need to make sure that we're ready for any eventuality, so each of you must look to your own section of the unit.'

Val hid a small smile as she realised that he reminded her a little of a general organising his army, then decided that it wasn't a bad analogy. If the worst happened and they were inundated with injuries, the hospital would resemble a battlefield and they would all end up waging a war against death.

After all their preparations it was something of an anti-climax when the rain stopped a little while later and the expected influx of casualties turned out to be a mere trickle.

'Thank God for small mercies,' Val muttered as she changed out of her borrowed uniform into her comfortably worn jeans and sweatshirt, and retrieved her coat and shoes.

'Tired?' Guy asked sympathetically as he pulled a thickly quilted jacket over the charcoal grey suit that seemed just as impeccable as when he'd left his home this morning.

'Well, put it this way—I'm glad that Berthe will have prepared a meal for us so all I have to do is sit down and eat. The thought of having to go home and cook a meal would be beyond me tonight.'

'I'm sorry, Val,' he said heavily. 'It isn't fair of me to ask you to do this. Would you rather stay at home tomorrow and rest?'

'While you're here having all this fun?' she demanded wryly. 'No. I'll see it through to the end. Apparently there were no new cases of flu among the staff today and some of the people who went down with it first are starting to come back to work. It looks as if the worst of your manpower—and womanpower—shortages will soon be over.'

Guy settled her in the comfort of the front seat and they started the now familiar journey back to the house that Val was beginning to think of as home.

Several times she pointed out places where the head-lights of the Citroën gleamed off unfamiliar stretches of water, some of them resembling fair-sized lakes.

'There's still quite a bit of water to add to that lot,' Guy commented as he flicked the windscreen wipers on to clear a scatter of drops.

'Why? We haven't had anything more than a sprinkle like that since the early part of the afternoon.'

'True. But that doesn't mean that we're not going to get the run-off from any rain that's fallen outside our area. It can take hours for that to arrive and swell what's been dumped directly on us here.'

'What was the forecast for this evening and tomorrow morning?' Val was beginning to realise that she'd been a bit premature in her relief.

'Isolated heavy showers with the possibility of thunderstorms,' he said. 'It's just a matter of luck where any of that will land. . .'

There was a sudden blinding flash of light which lit the area around them as brightly as day. The crash of the accompanying thunder was almost simultaneous and seemed to be centred directly above the roof of the car before the sound was drowned out by a deluge of water drumming down on the metal skin.

Visibility outside the car shrank to mere feet in spite of the bright headlights and the windscreen wipers going full pelt.

'I'm going to have to wait this out until it eases,' Guy called out over the cacophony and eased the car as close to the side of the road as he dared.

He left the engine running and tried to tune the radio to a local station to pick up any news of the extent of the storm, but the lightning was causing too much interference for anything to be intelligible.

'You said there would be isolated heavy showers,'

she commented. 'You didn't say that it would be our luck to get caught in one of them. . .'

She saw the gleam of his teeth in the darkness as he pulled a face at her and settled back in the relative warmth and comfort of the car.

The full fury of the storm lasted for nearly a quarter of an hour before Guy decided that the rain had eased enough for him to begin driving again. For most of that time the sound of the thunder and rain outside the car precluded any conversation but Val found that she didn't mind.

The realisation startled her and she was silently exploring the idea when another one slid into her thoughts—in spite of the storm raging around them she was perfectly content just to have the excuse to spend time in Guy's company.

She frowned, puzzled at the strange thoughts that would creep into a person's mind when they had time on their hands. . .

'Damn!' she heard Guy mutter and glanced out of the window just in time to see him halt the car with its bumper almost touching a fallen tree.

'Problem?'

'Big problem,' he confirmed as he reached for his mobile phone and began to tap out a code. 'I don't know if it was brought down by the rain or by lightning but it's completely blocking the road. . . Damn!' he repeated when the sound of static filled the interior of the car.

'Will we have to go back to the hospital?'

He was silent for a moment, one elbow braced on the steering-wheel while he rested his chin in his hand.

'I think I know a way. . .' he mused aloud, then, 'It's worth a try,' he said decisively and passed the phone across to her before he put the car into reverse gear and began to turn round. 'I'm going to try to rejoin the road by a back route which takes us along a slight ridge. I think it will be clear of floodwater and with any luck there won't be any fallen trees.'

'Don't mention luck,' Val warned. 'Last time it brought us a thunderstorm!'

'Impudent woman,' he accused. 'Make yourself useful. Find the repeat dial button on that thing and keep trying that number. We might get through as we climb the ridge.'

'And, if we do get through, who will be on the other end?'

'The police, so I can tell them about the blocked road. We don't want any emergency vehicles coming that way and getting stuck or, worse, ploughing into it. . .'

In between trying the mobile phone, Val was keeping a sharp eye out in case they encountered any more obstructions. She was hardly sparing the surrounding area any attention at all, knowing that there were more important things than scenery at the moment.

What it was that caught her eye just off the side of the road she didn't know, but something wasn't right.

'Stop,' she said sharply. 'Guy, stop the car!'

'Why?' he peered forward, his speed slowing immediately as he transferred his foot to the brake pedal.

'I think I saw something back there.' She twisted around in her seat, hampered by the bulk of her coat and the confines of the seat belt, then groaned when she realised that since they had moved past whatever she'd seen there was no light shining on it.

'What did you see?' Guy demanded as he brought the car to a halt. 'Was someone trying to flag us down?'

'No. I. . .I'm not certain exactly what it was, but I saw something that. . .' She shrugged, knowing that she was being horribly vague but still convinced that they ought to take a look. 'It was something that shouldn't have been there.'

'All right,' Guy agreed, and Val sighed with relief as he began to turn the car.

It wasn't nearly so easy on this road—it was much narrower and the edges weren't paved so that he had to be careful not to get the wheels stuck in the thick mud bordering the paved surface.

'How far back?' he demanded as he began retracing their route, his eyes flicking from the road ahead to the darkness outside the scope of their headlights.

'A bit further, near some bushes of some sort. . . There!' She pointed triumphantly as she caught sight of a bundle huddled under the pathetic shelter of the leafless thicket.

'It looks like something blown there by the wind— a fertiliser bag or something,' Guy said as he slowed the car right down and peered intently down the slope. 'It could even be some rubbish dumped by someone who couldn't be bothered to dispose of it properly.'

'Can we check?' Val pleaded, uncomfortably certain that there was something more than met the eye. 'Just in case?'

'On the understanding that if I get soaked and develop pneumonia, you will personally nurse me back to health,' he demanded as he angled the car so that the headlights fell directly on their quarry, and drew to a halt.

'Agreed,' she said with a chuckle, and watched keenly as he squelched his way carefully across the waterlogged strip of ground between the road and the shrubbery.

It only took him a second to look at the bundle before he was gesturing for Val to join him.

'Thank God for your sharp eyes,' he said as soon as she opened the car door, then called out a series of instructions so that it was several minutes before she joined him at the side of the road.

'Here's the blanket,' she said as she handed him the same plaid rug he'd used to wrap her in after she'd got soaked at the site of the plane crash. 'And here's your bag and the torch.'

'It's a young woman. . .' he began as she crouched down beside him. The words died away as he concentrated on examining her. 'A pregnant young woman with a plastic bag over her shoulders like a makeshift cape. . .'

There was a faint groan as he tried to wrap her in the blanket and the wet eyelashes flickered several times before they flew open with a rush.

'*Au secours*,' she whispered hoarsely, her trembling hands grasping feverishly at Guy as she gazed up at him, then groaned, '*Mon bébé. . .il vient . . .*'

CHAPTER SEVEN

SUDDENLY Val knew that it was going to be a very long night.

'Did she say her baby's coming?' she demanded over the sound of the returning rain. 'How long has she been in labour?'

She could hardly understand the poor woman's rambling words as Guy tried to decipher what she was saying, but in the end she decided she was more use to him if she concentrated on helping him to position her on the rug so that they could use it as a makeshift stretcher.

'Stay with her while I open the back out,' he directed. 'She'll be able to lie flat while we get her to the hospital.'

He'd been speaking in English as he scrambled his way up the bank but the young woman had obviously been listening and had recognised the last word.

'*Non! Non!*' She took her head wildly and when Val put a hand on her shoulder to try to calm her down she found the contact knocked away furiously and a stream of French hit her like hailstones, far too fast and far too disjointed for her to follow.

'What's going on?' Guy demanded as he rejoined the two of them.

'She says she's not going to the hospital but I can't understand the rest,' Val admitted. 'She's getting herself really worked up about something. She keeps mentioning her husband.'

Guy knelt down beside her, oblivious to the damage the mud and the rain were doing to his expensive clothing, and captured the woman's icy hands in his own.

'Gently! Gently! Calm down!' he crooned in French, and his husky voice brought back memories to Val of how he had soothed her after her nightmare.

Slowly and clearly he questioned the woman, whose name was Lise Sabatier, working on the assumption that her husband was going to be meeting her at the hospital for the birth of their child.

'*Non! Non! Il est blessé,*' she cried, becoming agitated all over again.

'*Il est à l'hôpital?*' Guy asked the obvious question when he heard that her husband was injured. Was this the reason why a heavily pregnant woman was wandering about in the dark in labour? Had her husband taken their only form of transport with him?

'*Non. Il est chez nous. Il y a eu un accident.*'

Val's heart sank. It didn't take much French to understand that it was her husband's accident which had sent her out into the rain to get help. What was Guy going to do?

'Release the catch on the front passenger seat so it's pushed back as far as it will go and then come back to help me lift her,' he said decisively. 'She's going to have to direct us to her home so that we can find out what's happened to her husband.'

'What about the baby?' Val prompted over her shoulder as she began to scramble up the slick slope.

'When the apple's ripe, it'll fall,' Guy murmured philosophically. 'She says it's only a few days early so, with any luck. . .'

'Don't you dare talk about luck,' she said fiercely as she finally straightened up at the edge of the road. 'With

the sort of luck you've been having this evening, we'll
end up having to deliver sextuplets by candlelight. . .'

His sharp bark of laughter sounded out of place in
the wet and the wind of their roadside rescue, but it
still brought an answering grin to her lips.

Once Guy had calmed Lise down enough to convince
her that they really were going to take her home, it was
the work of a few minutes before all three of them were
ensconced in the car.

For the third time Guy manoeuvred the vehicle in
what turned out to be a seven-point-turn, and set off
towards the farm.

From the narrow side road Lise soon directed them
down from the ridge on a smaller lane and eventually
onto a deeply rutted track which swooped between the
dark bulk of dimly seen trees.

'*Attention!*' she warned a few minutes later when the
headlights picked up the edge of a large body of water
which spread across the road and, almost in the middle,
the outline of a vehicle.

Guy inched his way past the stranded car, the deep
water washing a long way up the sides of his Citroën,
while their passenger explained how she'd managed to
coax the car through the deepest part but then the engine
had just died.

Val couldn't help marvelling at Lise's determination.

She'd had to abandon the car where it was, but had
waded through the rest of the water and continued on
foot for a further two miles to try to fetch help for her
husband. Val was willing to bet that the young woman
might even have succeeded if the storm hadn't caused
her to lose her footing in the slick mud at the side of
the road and crash down the slope.

Her eyes flew to the illuminated clock on the car

dashboard when a soft moan told her that Lise's next contraction had started.

'Six minutes,' she muttered to Guy from her position in the seat behind him, and saw him nod his comprehension.

'*Par là,*' Lise groaned through her pain and pointed to a neatly repaired gateway.

The farmhouse at the end of the driveway was in total darkness as they pulled up outside it, and Lise immediately began to struggle to get out of the car.

Once again it was left to Guy to try to talk some sense into her and Val heard him stressing the importance of her baby and trying to persuade her to wait for them in the car.

Val had escaped the dark confines of the vehicle as soon as possible, ready to lend a hand wherever it was needed.

As she stood in the yard beside the car she grimaced ruefully at the fact that she was soaking wet again and flicked raindrops off her nose as she leant forward to try to hear what Guy was saying.

In the dim illumination of the car's courtesy light she could see very little of their passenger except the fact that she had managed to turn in the seat and now had her feet on the ground, her arms waving as she either argued with Guy or was explaining where to find her husband.

Val gave up her attempts at eavesdropping and straightened up again to peer around.

She'd had a brief glimpse of the farmhouse and its surroundings when the car headlights had swept over them, but the appalling weather and the lack of lights in the house meant that there was almost nothing discernible in the wild, wet night.

She turned round slowly in a complete circle, trying to imagine—from the few shapes she could make out— what sort of place they'd come to, unable to stop the quiver of unease which travelled the length of her spine as the hated darkness pressed in around them.

It almost seemed as if they had arrived on a film set for a story set a century ago: the period farmhouse set in a clearing and surrounded by trees—she could even smell the smoke from the open fires they would use to heat it and do the cooking. . .

It was the dull orange glow outlining one corner of the farmhouse which brought her out of her imaginings, and she suddenly realised that she could smell a *real* fire.

'Did Lise light a fire before she left to get help?' she interrupted loudly, pointing in the direction of the swiftly growing patch of light.

Lise gave a piercing scream and struggled frantically to push Guy aside.

'Val! Keep her out of the way!' Guy ordered as he abandoned Lise into her care and raced across the farmyard towards the ominous glow.

Val was no match for a woman who believed her man was in danger.

Lise was barely five feet two and heavily pregnant, but in spite of all Val's efforts the best she could do to follow Guy's orders was to hang onto the frantic young woman's arm as she lumbered in his wake.

They rounded the corner side by side and gasped in unison at the sight that met their eyes.

One of the farm buildings had obviously been repaired for use as a workshop but one side of it was now engulfed in flames, with the first few tongues beginning to lick their way through a corner of the roof.

'Jean,' Lise screamed, fighting against Val's tight hold on her arm. '*Il est dedans. . .*'

Guy was just a black outline silhouetted against the rapidly growing conflagration, one arm thrown up in front of his face for protection while he circled the burning building trying to peer through the flames.

Val's heart leapt into her mouth when she suddenly realised that he was going to try to find a way past the flames to rescue the trapped man, and she suddenly knew what Lise was feeling.

It wouldn't take much for her to scream Guy's name and rush forward to try to stop him from risking his life too.

'*Un seau, Lise,*' she snapped loudly, the urgency of her demand cutting the young woman off in mid-scream. '*Et de l'eau.*'

For a second Lise hesitated, obviously torn between her desire to rescue her man and to direct Val to the things she needed to help.

'*La.*' She pointed, her eyes suddenly clear and determined as she led Val at a lumbering run towards the back door of the house.

Two buckets had been turned upside down beside the stone steps and Val swooped to grab one in each hand before she raced towards the water trough just yards away.

She'd heard about people who performed amazing feats in emergency situations but, until she scooped up two full buckets of water and ran across the yard with them, she'd never really believed them.

'Guy!' she shrieked over the growing noise of the fire as he approached the flaming entrance of the shed at an angle. 'Wait!' And she put the second bucket

down to take a grip with her free hand on the bottom
of the first one.

'Wet yourself first!' she shouted over the
frightening roar.

She paused as he took a step towards her then held
his arms out by his sides while she threw half of the
bucketful at his chest, repeating the exercise when he
turned his back towards her.

The second bucket was swiftly retrieved and the full
contents sent in a gleaming arc to splatter down the
edge of the doorway and across the floor of the shed.

For just a brief moment the water made a dark path
through the searing flames and she could see a huddled
figure inside the shed.

'Again!' Guy shouted and Val whirled and ran to
collect another load, sending each of them in through
the doorway of the shed.

In the split second after the last stream landed Guy
ran through the gap it made in the fiery opening and
was swallowed up inside.

Val bit back the terrified moan that rose up in her
throat and ran back to fill the buckets again, peering
vainly through the brief window in the flames to see if
Guy was safe before she repeated the procedure—again
and again.

'Where are they? Where are they?' she was sobbing
breathlessly as she scooped up the next two bucketfuls
and turned back towards the shed, her arms feeling as
if they, too, were on fire as she flung the water with
all her dwindling strength.

Even as the flames died down a little in response to
the repeated drenching Val could see that the fire was
going to win in the end. Now it wasn't just one side of
the shed and a corner of the roof affected but the whole

structure, the flames licking greedily up the roof from the back of the shed too.

As she braced herself to throw the next load there was an ominous groaning and she watched in horror as, in apparent slow motion, one side of the roof caved in and the wall began to follow it down.

'No!' Val shrieked despairingly as she began to run towards the shed, the heavy bucket all but forgotten in her hand as she suddenly realised just how much Guy had come to mean to her. How could it be that she was watching him go to his death before her stupid heart admitted that she was in love with him?

She was close enough to the fire for her eyes to feel as if they were singeing when she imagined she saw a dark shadow moving somewhere in the depths of the conflagration.

Without thinking, she swung the bucket forward and flung its contents towards the wavering shape.

Mere seconds after the water penetrated the curtain of flames a strange creature burst through the dim path she had made and lurched forward several paces before it collapsed in a heap on the ground.

Her heart and her mind were at war so that she was torn between racing forward to see who had come to safety and grabbing more water to douse the smouldering heap of humanity. Logic won and she whirled away again and filled the buckets for the last time, staggering forward with the dead weight dragging her arms almost out of their sockets and dumping each bucket over the dark heap.

'Jean?' Lise sobbed as she scurried forward to join Val. '*C'est Jean?*' and she bent forward awkwardly and dropped to her knees to try to roll the figure over.

'Is he alive?' croaked Guy's voice as he lifted his

head out of the sea of mud surrounding him and tipped his burden off his shoulders. 'Can you get him further away from the fire?'

Val's heart leapt with joy.

He was alive.

Guy was alive.

'Val?' he growled weakly. 'Help me get us out of here!'

'Of course!' she whispered through a throat grown tight with suppressed tears, and sped across the brightly lit clearing to retrieve the pathetic bundle of plaid fabric lying where the young woman had dropped it in her dash to help her husband.

'This car rug was certainly worth every penny you paid for it,' she joked brokenly as the two of them carefully rolled the semi-conscious man onto it to carry him into the house, leaving the fire to burn itself out.

'He was pinned down inside the shed by a stack of timber that had become wedged in position,' Guy explained hoarsely as the two of them checked their latest patient over. 'The initial impact had broken his leg so it was almost impossible to get any leverage.

'In the end it was the collapse of the side of the shed which shifted the timber and allowed me to pull him out, but by then I couldn't see where the doorway was—until you sent that last lot of water in my face.'

'Anything to oblige,' Val said, blinking back tears when she realised just how close to disaster he had come. 'In the meantime I think we're going to have to leave Jean to cope by himself for a minute. We'll have to give our attention to Lise until we've made certain how she's getting on.'

During a lull in the weather Guy finally managed to

telephone a message through to Berthe to contact the police, and Val could see how relieved he was when the down-to-earth woman promised to stay with his grandmother overnight.

The next hour was spent alternately with Lise, as she progressed rapidly towards the culmination of her first labour, and with Jean, who needed a splint to be fixed to his broken leg and dressings on the worst of his burns.

'Lise is blaming herself for the whole thing,' Val reported in a hushed voice as she handed Guy the cup of coffee she'd just made on the other side of the kitchen.

In spite of its size the kitchen was so delightfully warm that they'd decided to make it their unofficial hospital ward, the old-fashioned stove serving not only as a source of heat for cooking and comfort but also supplying hot water in abundance.

Making the coffee had been Val's first experience of using a solid fuel stove and she'd felt almost like the characters she'd imagined living here when she'd first seen the house.

'How on earth can she be to blame?' Guy objected with a frown, bringing Val back to their original conversation. 'She risked her own life and that of her unborn baby when she went to get help for him.'

'But she lit the lantern and left it with him in case it got dark before she came back. She didn't want him to regain consciousness in the dark.' She hoped her own shudder wasn't visible in the shadowy kitchen.

'She wasn't to know that Jean would come to and start trying to clear the stack while he was still underneath it. It was just sheer chance that one length of timber fell and knocked the lamp over.'

'How's he doing now?' Val murmured as they went

back to their patients. 'Is he still refusing painkillers for his injuries?'

'I managed to persuade him to let me give him something to deaden the pain in his leg, provided I swore that it wouldn't make him go to sleep. He's just so lucky that he was lying on the floor of the shed with plenty of gaps between the boards for ventilation. I don't think he's inhaled any more smoke than during the length of time it took to carry him out.'

'He's determined he's going to be with Lise when the baby's born, isn't he? You certainly slowed him down when you splinted his legs together.'

She looked across at the two of them, one lying on a low divan they'd carried through from another room and the other on a makeshift mattress on the floor, their fingers entwined as he murmured encouragingly to her.

'Well, at least this way I can be sure that he's staying where we put him and not doing any further damage to his leg.'

'It shouldn't be long now—she was almost fully dilated when I checked a few minutes ago,' Val reported.

'Well.' Guy tipped the heavy pottery mug to drain the last mouthful, then threw her one of his wicked grins. 'We might be dealing with lanterns instead of candles, but let's see about these sextuplets you promised me.'

The healthy lifestyle and frequent exercise Lise had been having throughout her pregnancy must have stood her in good stead because it was less than half an hour later that her son drew his first breath and let it out in a lusty yell.

'He's beautiful,' Val said reverently as she lifted him

up and laid him on his mother's stomach, and the words needed no translation.

Val helped to prop Jean up so that the new parents could admire their precious baby together for a moment before she took him away to wrap him up safe and warm while Guy completed the delivery process.

'What's the next step?' Val asked when she'd finished making Lise comfortable and had settled little André in the cradle Jean had carved for him. 'Should we transport the three of them to the hospital?'

'Not tonight,' Guy murmured quietly. 'I don't want to take any more chances in the dark—especially with the baby. If we got stuck for any reason. . .'

For the first time she could hear in his voice how tired he was and her heart went out to him.

There hadn't been any time for him to recover from the trauma of being trapped in the fire before he was having to concentrate his expertise and energy on an injured man and a young woman in labour.

He'd been a tower of strength to the young couple and to Val, without a thought for himself.

'You need some sleep,' she said, her tone decisive in spite of the fact that they were whispering. 'It's time to find you a bed so you can get your head down for a while.'

'That could be a problem,' he warned, his dark gaze serious as he faced her in the mellow light. 'In fact, there are several problems so I'd better begin at the beginning and explain.'

He drew in a deep breath and rubbed the palms of his hands down his face, then winced as he found the place where a piece of blazing timber had seared him. A patch of his beard had been singed right off to show an angry mark.

Val had insisted on treating it but he'd hardly allowed her time to do more than check the severity of the burn before he'd tried to dismiss it as unimportant.

It had been Lise who had directed Val to the aloe vera plant growing in a pot on the kitchen window-sill and told her to smear the juice from its inner flesh on the burn—a natural remedy she had used very successfully in the past.

'Jean and Lise were telling me that this is a long-term project for them,' Guy told Val. 'They are gradually refurbishing the house by their own efforts and doing without what they can't have straight away—hence using lamps until they can afford to run new electricity cable through the house.'

'Really!' Val was amazed. The house was even closer to her original idea than she'd imagined. 'I thought they'd got the lanterns out because of a power failure.'

He smiled briefly at her enthusiasm, then continued.

'They've got one lantern in here, which we'll need to check up on them during the night, but Lise took their second one out to the shed for Jean.'

'And?' Val knew he was trying to tell her something but couldn't immediately see what it was.

'Their only other means of lighting is candles, and, apart from the two stumps over beside the stove, their entire stock of candles went up when the fire burnt the temporary store-room at one end of the shed.'

'But. . .' Her throat went dry at the thought of the darkness surrounding this one haven of light.

'The other problem is the fact that there's only one room with a bed in it,' he said baldly.

She could feel her eyes widen as she stared at him in shock, half expecting his serious expression to dissolve into the familiar wicked grin—but it didn't.

'I can't... We can't...' She shook her head as she stammered and stumbled amid her whirling thoughts.

'We need to get some sleep,' he continued firmly. 'We don't know what situation we'll find ourselves in tomorrow and, after single-handedly shifting half the volume of a medium-sized swimming-pool, you need some rest.'

'But... How are we going to...? Where will we...?' She gave up, closing her mouth tightly to hide the trembling of her lips.

She was so confused by the double blow he had just dealt her that she didn't know whether she was more afraid of the fact that if she left the kitchen she was going to end up being plunged into the darkness she feared so much, or whether it was the idea that she was going to have to share a bed with Guy before she'd had a chance to come to terms with her recognition of her feelings for him.

'Come and have a look,' he invited her quietly, reaching for one of the candles in its little hand-thrown pottery holder.

As easily as if he'd been doing it for years, he took a spill from the container on the back of the stove, touched it to the glowing coals behind the fire door and transferred the flame to the candle wick.

Within seconds it was glowing strongly and, with a brief word for the young couple, he led Val out into the hallway.

'It's in here,' he announced as he pushed open a polished door, the wood gleaming richly in the buttery light. 'What do you think?'

'It's a four-poster bed!' Val exclaimed in delight and crossed to examine the carved posts at each corner.

'Jean made this, didn't he? The carving is the same as on the cradle he made for André.'

'And the quilt on it was hand-made by Lise and all the bed-linen was fresh this morning,' he said quietly. 'But that doesn't solve *your* problems, does it?'

'Problems?' She turned towards him and saw the way the candle he held in one lean hand highlighted the loss of one side of his beard and the injury to his face, and her stomach clenched at the graphic reminder of how close he had come to death this evening.

'I know about your problem with darkness and enclosed spaces,' he prompted. 'And if there was any way to change the situation we're in—'

'I'm sorry, Guy,' Val broke in, her voice conveying a determination she wasn't sure she could maintain but she was certainly going to give it a try... 'I'm a grown woman, for heaven's sake. I'll be able to manage for one night...'

She hoped he couldn't hear the tremor in her voice and raised her chin another notch in compensation.

'Would it help if we tried the same remedy as last time?' he offered, and this time she could see the wicked glint in his eyes.

'Remedy?' she challenged, her heart beginning a rapid tattoo against her ribs as she guessed what was coming.

'Well, we both need to rest,' he began, his tone the essence of logic as he ticked the points off with his fingers. 'And there's only one bed, and you need some-one there to hold you in the dark, so I would have thought the answer was obvious.'

'Would you?' she said, tamping down the urge to laugh aloud. 'I think your offer is amazingly generous and I do thank you for it, but I couldn't possibly put you to the trouble of—'

'Dammit, woman, come here,' he growled, his voice huskier than ever as he reached for her with his free hand and pulled her against him. 'I can't tell in this light how much of what you're saying is sheer bravado, but I wish you'd give me the chance to take care of you.' He rested his cheek on her hair, cradling her head against the solid warmth of his shoulder.

Val's arms crept around his waist and she sighed as a delicious feeling of comfort and security enveloped her.

'On condition that you give me a chance to take care of you in return,' she murmured softly, tilting her head up to brush a feather-light kiss as close as she dared to the angry mark on his cheek.

'Val?' He lifted her chin so that their eyes met, his own once more intent. 'You don't have to worry that I'll take advantage of the situation.'

'I know. I can trust you,' she said simply and smiled.

A swift frown appeared between the dark crescents of his eyebrows and she nearly chuckled. He hadn't expected her to say that, had he. . .?

'If you don't mind waiting,' she continued smartly, 'I'd like to borrow the candle to visit the bathroom before we settle down for the night. . .'

The next few minutes were taken up with a quick wash, interrupted by longing looks at the shower. After the soaking and all the frantic exercise today it was a torment to know that, thanks to the boiler incorporated in the kitchen stove, there would be endless blissfully hot water—if only she could take advantage of it.

Firmly she put it out of her mind and thought instead of the young couple in the kitchen.

Jean had finally consented to another dose of

analgesic to help him rest, but Lise needed no help. The physical and mental stress she'd been under for the last twelve hours, first in her desperate attempts to rescue her husband and then to bring her baby into the world, meant that she was already dead to the world.

Val took a last look at her wavering reflection in the mirror over the basin and pulled a wry face. The repeated soaking had done little more than leave her gamine hairstyle looking a bit limp and bedraggled— nothing that a session with shampoo and hot water wouldn't cure. It was the pale face and huge dark eyes staring out at her which would take a bit longer to return to normal. . .

She tried to shrug and winced at the stiff muscles, turning her back on her less than glamorous image as she took the candle into the bedroom and placed it carefully on the makeshift bedside table and then gingerly sat down on the side of the bed with her open hands resting on her lap.

Her hands were still stinging from the contact of soap in the blisters torn open by the bucket handles but that would soon fade—unlike the electric thrumming along her nerves which was increasing with every passing second.

In spite of the ever-present sound of the wind in the surrounding trees, the house was silent enough that she could hear Guy in the kitchen as he gave a last top-up of fuel to the stove and then she heard his husky voice as he reminded Jean that the two of them were only a shout away.

She heard him shut the kitchen door to keep the baby warm but as he began to make his way along the corridor towards the room they were about to share there was no sound at all from his sock-clad feet, and her pulse began to race at the thought of his silent approach.

Even in the chill of the shadowy room she could feel a gradual heat rise up her throat and into her cheeks, half embarrassment and half unwilling arousal, as she visualised what the next few minutes might bring.

CHAPTER EIGHT

'WHY aren't you in bed?' Guy whispered, his eyes seeming darker than ever in the shadows on the other side of the room as he closed the door and turned to face Val.

'Because the sheets are freezing!' she hissed back, glad that he was too far away to see the betraying heat in her cheeks. *They* were nearly hot enough to make toast.

'So what are you expecting *me* to do?' he demanded as he stalked towards her with a fluid predator's stride. 'Get in and warm them up for you?'

'I thought you'd never offer,' she replied cheekily in spite of her nerves. 'I can't seem to find the electric blanket and I forgot to bring my fluffy pink bedsocks.'

'Bedsocks!' He sounded so horrified that she was hard put not to giggle. 'I have never been to bed with a woman who wears bedsocks!'

'Well, now's your chance,' she offered brightly. 'I haven't got them with me, but at least you'll be able to say you've been to bed with a woman who wears them. . .' Then she spoiled the effect of her light-hearted prattling by shivering—he wasn't to know that it was due to nerves rather than the chill of the room.

She was certain that the mumbled words he was saying as he deposited his wallet and watch beside the candle-holder and began to undo the buttons of his shirt were words of disgust, but she didn't comment—all her energy was concentrated on remembering to breathe as he nonchalantly stripped off his shirt and revealed a glowing bronze torso which was every bit as broad and muscular as she had imagined.

'Aren't you going to take your outside clothes off at least?' he prompted when he sat down uncomfortably close on the edge of the bed to remove his socks.

'Um. . . That's a bit of a problem,' she mumbled and clasped one hand uneasily in the other, ignoring the renewed sting in her palms as her knuckles whitened with tension.

'What problem?' He half turned towards her and out of the corner of her eye she caught a glimpse of the way the candlelight highlighted individual strands of the tangle of dense dark hair spreading from one male nipple to the other.

As she watched she saw him straighten up and reach for the waistband of his trousers and dragged her eyes away from his body and her mind back to what she was saying.

'I can't,' she blurted out, and the hand which had just reached down to grasp the tab of his zip froze.

He stayed very still for a second and then subsided slowly on to the edge of the bed again, almost as though she was a timid forest animal and would be frightened by any sudden move.

'But you said. . .' he began sharply and then paused, and she heard him draw in a steadying breath. 'You said you trusted me.' There was hurt in his tone and she realised that he had misunderstood.

'I trust you more than you know,' she said emphatically, finally finding the courage to meet his eyes. 'What I was actually trying to tell you just now was that I can't take my clothes off because I'm too sore—from carrying the buckets.'

She couldn't be sure but she thought he sighed as he

reached out for the hands now lying limply in her lap. She'd been telling the truth when she'd said she trusted him, and just repeating the words aloud had dissolved all the tension.

'Your poor hands,' he murmured and raised each of them towards the candlelight for a close inspection before he startled her by gently kissing them. 'I didn't thank you for saving my life,' he said huskily. 'If you hadn't kept fetching that water and throwing it. . .' He shook his head, his dark eyes very intent as they roamed over her face—their touch almost physical as they reached her lips.

Val longed to reach for him, to draw his head towards hers so that he could satisfy the longing he had awoken with just a glance, but she forced herself to watch silently as several expressions followed each other fleetingly across his face until he blinked as if he was waking from a dream.

'Come on,' he murmured, a touch of gravel in his husky tones. 'You need to sleep. . .' And he reached for the hem of her sweatshirt.

'Ahh. . .!' she groaned as her shoulders complained at the movement. 'Slowly. . .!'

'What on earth. . .?' he exclaimed. 'What did I do? Did I knock your hands?'

'It's my shoulders,' she moaned. 'They've stiffened up on me and I can't seem to. . .'

'Bloody woman,' he grumbled under his breath as he urged her off the bed, reaching out one long arm to grab the rapidly shrinking candle before he shepherded her towards the door. 'Why didn't you tell me you were in pain?'

'I wasn't,' she hissed as he pushed her out into the silence of the dark hallway, conscious that her voice might disturb the occupants of the kitchen. 'The pain only came when I stopped moving. . . What are you doing?' she squeaked as he pushed the bathroom door open.

'Putting you under the shower,' he announced shortly, his expression grim.

'But. . .' Her eyes flew wide open as his words registered.

'Don't argue,' he warned as he reached once again for the hem of her sweatshirt and began to ease it up towards her shoulders. 'You know very well that you'll be even worse in the morning if you don't do something about it now.' He carefully stretched the fabric to release one shoulder, then the other.

His actions were as calm and matter-of-fact as if she was just another patient as he drew the fleece-lined cloth over her head and folded the garment neatly before he reached for the buttons marching down the front of her shirt.

He might be unaffected by what he was doing, Val thought crossly as he peeled the soft fabric down her arms, but every square millimetre of her skin was aware that he was gradually removing every stitch of her clothing.

She was standing in her matching ecru bra and pants when he paused to turn the water on, checking the temperature carefully, before he returned to his task and whisked her remaining scraps of covering away and assisted her calmly under the pounding spray.

'Ooh! That feels so good. . .!' she moaned softly, closing her eyes in bliss as she tilted her head forward to allow the hot water to pummel the strained muscles stretching up from her shoulder into her neck.

For several long moments she was oblivious to

anything but the blessed relief of the warmth seeping
its way into every fibre of her abused body—until two
hands took a firm hold of her shoulders.

'Guy!' she squeaked, rigid with shock, and ended up
with a faceful of water when she tried to turn. 'What
are you. . .? I thought you'd gone back to the bedroom.'

'Stop wriggling,' he ordered, tightening his grip so
that she was unable to move out of the stream of water
as he began to work his thumbs in soothing circles over
her knotty muscles. 'Let me give you some relief.'

There was relief and there was relief, Val thought
fatalistically as she surrendered to his ministrations, hating and loving in equal amounts the punishment he was
putting her through.

As he worked his way around the shoulder girdle of
each arm she wasn't certain at first whether the agony
of the treatment was worth the easing of the stiffness
it was bringing, but the longer he went on the less it
felt like a physical punishment and the more it felt like
a test of mental endurance.

His touch was magic. Each stroke furthered the relief
she needed if she wasn't going to be crippled by the
morning, but it also increased the pleasure she was
deriving from having his hands touch her, stroke her,
caress her—each movement magnified by the silky
lubrication of warm water and soapy lather.

How much longer?

The words were a silent scream as she gritted her
teeth and concentrated on locking her knees, knowing
that they were in imminent danger of allowing her to
collapse into a heap.

'Val. . .?' Guy's voice was a hoarse groan that
stroked her nerves like thick velvet over sandpaper and
she leaned back against the pressure of his hands, her

head tipping back helplessly so that the water poured down on her face—and she hardly noticed, conscious only of the naked arms which had suddenly circled her from behind and pulled her back against an equally naked male body.

'Ah, Val,' he groaned again, his voice right beside her ear as her head came to rest on his shoulder. He tightened his grasp and they came into contact along the full length of their bodies, their planes and hollows fitting together like the two complementary halves of a whole.

'I've been thinking about this,' he murmured as his hands shaped her ribs and stroked the smooth curve of her waist as if he was appreciating a fine piece of sculpture, then retraced his path and continued upwards—towards the yearning flesh of her breasts.

'You. . .have?' she questioned on a gasp as he finally cupped both hands around her, his thumbs curving inward to strum her nipples into pouting arousal.

'Even when I was surrounded by fire,' he admitted hoarsely as one hand went exploring on its own and found a fire of a different kind. 'When it looked as if I might not survive the only regret that came to mind was that I hadn't told you how I feel about you; hadn't held you naked in my arms and made love to you. . .'

Val turned her head towards him, her heart full to overflowing as she searched for his mouth, needing his kiss more than she needed her next breath.

When he turned her in his arms so that her nipples felt the rough abrasion of the thick dark hair on his chest she murmured in delight, swaying slightly to increase the friction and raising her arms to wrap them around him—desperate to hold him as tightly as he was holding her.

'Ouch. . .' she moaned as her shoulders protested, and her heart sank as Guy immediately stopped his exploration of the silky globes of her bottom.

'What are we doing?' he muttered with open dismay in his tone, and her heart fell still further when his hands left her body completely.

Without daring to look up at the expression on his face, she stepped away from him, turning to grab a towel to cover her nakedness as he reached out to turn off the shower.

What a fool, she berated herself as she clumsily tried to wrap the length of cloth around her without catching her sore hands and realising wryly that she'd completely forgotten about the raw blisters when he'd been kissing her.

What on earth did she think she was doing?

If Guy hadn't come to his senses, embarrassing as it was, she'd been willing to forget everything to stay in his arms in spite of the fact that to have made love with Guy—a man she'd only met a few short days ago— would have gone against everything she believed in. . .

'Here. . .' Guy's husky voice interrupted her censuring thoughts as he took the towel from her and wrapped it around her. The fact that she might have misunderstood his reaction to their lovemaking only dawned on her when, instead of quickly knotting the ends to cover her nakedness, he held the edges apart to frame her body as he ran hot eyes over every inch of her.

'Guy?' she began uncertainly as the doused remains of the fire of her arousal began to smoulder again.

Her voice drew his dark eyes up to lock with hers and the fire instantly began to rage out of control. No one had ever looked at her like that—as if she was the most beautiful, the most desirable woman in the world.

'Ah, Valentine Burgess, I need you,' he said, his voice deep and impassioned as he said the words in his native language. 'I think I will go mad if I can't take you to bed tonight. . .this instant!'

'I think we will both go mad—or freeze—if we don't go to bed this instant,' she retorted, sudden nervousness making her wrap the towel awkwardly over her shivering body. 'This is February, after all, and it's definitely not the time of year for parading around naked.'

Grateful for the momentary reprieve, she took advantage of his stunned expression and brushed past him, grabbing the guttering candle and scampering along the corridor on bare feet until she reached the sanctuary of their bedroom.

The instant she caught sight of the magnificent four-poster she regretted her cowardice, but it was too late. She had spoilt the mood. . .

'Is this truly how you feel?' Guy demanded hoarsely, obviously having difficulty remembering to keep his voice down when he followed her a moment later.

The bundle of clothes he'd paused to retrieve from the bathroom was piled haphazardly in his arms as he glared at her across the room, apparently totally unaware that he had forgotten his own towel. 'Are you Englishwomen so pragmatic that you can see the prospect of going to bed with your lover as a remedy for cold weather?'

Val nearly giggled with relief when she saw his outraged expression but knew better than to give in to the temptation. She'd learnt many years ago that the male ego was a very fragile flower.

She turned to face him, her heart beginning to beat faster and her icy toes curled nervously into the hand-knotted bedside rug as she steeled herself for the step she was about to take.

'I don't know about other Englishwomen, Guy,' she said softly, 'but *this* one needs some help to dry her hair.'

Briefly she flicked an admiring gaze down the long length of his powerfully muscled legs and back up again, her attention pausing for an extra moment on the dark thicket at the juncture of his thighs and the burgeoning evidence of his potent masculinity.

'As you appear to have forgotten to bring a towel from the bathroom I suppose I'll have to ask you to use mine instead,' she finished as she released the half-hearted knot which barely held the towel at her breasts and allowed it to unwind itself from her body, retaining her grasp of one corner to hold it out towards Guy in invitation.

There were several long seconds of silence and her cheeks started to burn with embarrassment as he just stood looking at her, his expression inscrutable in the wavering candlelight.

Before either of them could move the candle gave a final gutter and died, plunging the room into utter darkness.

After her initial shriek of shock Val became paralysed with fear, her throat closing up so that she could barely breathe.

'Val?' The concern in Guy's voice hardly penetrated the panic which filled her. 'Sweetheart, I'm coming. . . Don't be frightened. . . Damn!' There was a thump in the darkness and several less than gentlemanly curses as his voice drew closer. 'Where are you, my love. . .?'

As soon as his hand brushed her shoulder she

flinched, but the numb paralysis was broken and she threw herself into his arms.

'Oh, Guy! Thank God you're here.' She burrowed frantically against him as he wrapped his arms around her, granting her the security she needed. 'It's so dark,' she whispered, hating the pathetic sound of her voice.

'Does it matter?' he murmured against her ear, nuzzling his way down her neck.

'Matter? Of course it matters,' she insisted tearfully.

'Why? Do you make love with your eyes open?'

'Do I. . .what?' She was startled by the direction the conversation had taken and it showed.

'Well, I know that when we kiss you close your eyes,' he explained as patiently as if she were a small child. 'So I want to know if you keep your eyes open when you make love—because if I kiss you while we make love your eyes will stay closed so you won't even know if it's dark.'

Val couldn't help it; the giggle sneaked out when she was still speechless at his nonsense, and he took advantage of her distraction to swing her up into his arms and move forward cautiously to lay her on the bed.

'Get under the covers—quickly,' he urged, and followed her swiftly between the icy sheets, turning her towards him and wrapping her quivering body tightly in his arms.

'I'm sorry the candle went out,' he whispered as he stroked one palm up and down her back. 'Sorry that you were frightened but more sorry that it stops me from seeing you.'

He cupped one hand around her cheek and turned her face up towards his, finding her lips unerringly in spite of the darkness.

'Close your eyes,' he murmured, the words a soft

caress against her lips as she obeyed. 'Now, use your other eyes to see,' he instructed and showed her how, his husky voice filling the cosy space under the covers with his glowing description of the way he saw her body—from her gamine hairstyle and big dark eyes to the pale perfection of her breasts and long slender legs, while his clever fingers explored and caressed each of them.

'Now it's your turn,' he prompted, and she could hear the wicked smile in his voice. 'I know you took your own sweet time ogling me, so. . .'

'Ogling!' she said haughtily, her voice trembling for an entirely different reason. 'I never ogle.'

'In which case I feel very privileged that I was the object of your first attempt, and may I congratulate you on how well you did it!'

Another giggle escaped her and she buried her face against his neck.

'Well?' he prompted.

'Well, what?'

'Did you like what you saw?' he demanded in mock outrage.

She thought about teasing him, but suddenly she knew that the time for teasing was over.

'Yes,' she said quietly. 'I liked what I saw very much.' She ran her fingertips over the width of his shoulders and down onto his chest, delighting in the way the thick dark hair clung to her.

Her exploration led her to discover that his tight male nipples were just as sensitive as her own, in spite of their size, and she was just about to test that theory further by following the silky hair which narrowed its way down over the taut muscles of his stomach when he captured her hands gently in his.

'Val. . .please. . .I need you too badly to stand much more of that. . .'

She was amazed to hear the tension in his voice. She hadn't really understood until now that his attraction to her was just as all-encompassing as hers was to him.

'I need you badly, too,' she admitted. 'I need to feel you close so that I know that I didn't lose you in the fire; I need to feel you holding me so that I can feel safe from all my stupid fears; but, most of all, I need to feel you making love to me so that I can feel whole. . .'

The last word barely emerged before his mouth mated with hers in a kiss full of the promise of how it would be when their bodies were joined and she welcomed him, opening her mouth to him as eagerly as she offered her body for the ultimate consummation.

Several times in the night Guy got up to check on Lise and baby André, and to top up Jean's analgesics.

Each time he returned Val was waiting for him in the dark, which held few terrors for her now. When he shed his clothes she greeted him with open arms, wrapping him in her warmth while he reciprocated by arousing her to heights of passion she'd never known before.

Finally she woke when the pre-dawn greyness was seeping into the room and saw Guy's face beside her on the pillow for the first time.

She savoured the opportunity to gaze her fill, admiring the shape of his head and the thick head of hair in so dark a brown that it was almost black. His beard was very dark, too, and the closely cropped style followed the line of his jaw without obscuring its strength.

The angry burn which had marred one cheek last night was hardly visible in the half-light, its position only made obvious by the glaring absence of the hair which had been burnt away.

Val wondered, briefly, what he would do about his beard. Would he trim all of it much shorter until the new growth caught up, or would his professionalism demand that he should look neat and force him to shave it all off?

She leant a little closer, trying to imagine what Guy would look like without his beard, and was captured by two warm arms.

'*Bonjour*,' he murmured throatily, and rolled her over to deliver a leisurely kiss.

'*Bonjour*,' she echoed, and tightened her arms around his shoulders. She knew that soon they would have to leave the comfort and temporary security of this magnificent bed but she couldn't help trying to delay the moment as long as possible, revelling in the feeling of lying with Guy's arms around her and marvelling at how right it felt—as if he was the other half of her. . .

A forceful wail drifted along the corridor and intruded on their peace.

'That sounds like our wake-up call,' Guy joked as he tightened his arm briefly about her shoulders.

'I suppose that means it's time we thought about transporting them to hospital,' Val forced herself to comment lightly as she slid reluctantly out of his arms, half hoping that he would prevent her from going.

'Still, if you were right about the flu epidemic slowing down perhaps we'll be lucky enough to get some time off. . .' Guy began.

'Don't you start talking about luck again,' she ordered. 'We've had enough trouble with that already!'

She slid her feet over the side of the bed and fished with her toes for Guy's shirt, pulling it on before she stood up. After her blatant display last night she felt strangely shy about him seeing her naked this morning—as if the ultimate intimacies they had shared meant that more than her body would be revealed now.

'Spoilsport,' he accused huskily, his lean body sprawled halfway across the bed like one of the big cats, apparently boneless in relaxation but with the potential for instant powerful action. 'I was looking forward to a repeat of last night's show, but in reverse order,' he continued, his voice deepening until it made her think of dark brown velvet brushing over her skin.

The combination of his words and her thoughts made her blush and he chuckled wickedly.

There was still a sizeable lake of water surrounding the Sabatiers' stranded car when Guy eased his Citroën past it again, but at least it seemed as if there would be no more rain for a while and it was a far easier job in daylight.

After a delicious breakfast of Lise's home-made bread and conserves and a large pot of heavenly coffee, Val and Guy had managed to organise a temporary pallet in the back of the car, the rear seat folded out of the way to allow their patients to travel in some degree of comfort.

Guy threw Val a wry smile as they heard Lise apologising to Jean for flooding the car but, apart from the occasional murmured word, Jean kept his reassurances private.

'You managed to get through to the emergency services on your mobile phone, I take it?'

'Eventually.' Guy nodded. 'I reached them just after midnight and told them the complete tale of woe. They asked if we needed rescuing immediately but I told them we'd make it under our own steam in the morning—they had enough to do with keeping the roads clear and dealing with real emergencies among the evacuees.'

'Were they able to bring you up to date with the situation at the hospital?' she enquired, amazed that she hadn't thought to ask before. It was almost as if they had stepped into a different world when they had arrived at the Sabatiers' farm—a place where time stood still.

'Everything was OK at the time they were speaking, but you know as well as I do that the situation can change in minutes.'

'Calm efficiency to chaos in one easy lesson,' she quipped just as she recognised a familiar road and realised that they were only moments away from the hospital.

Thanks to Guy's mobile phone, Lise's relatives had been informed about the events of the last twenty-four hours and would be arriving at some stage to take care of transporting the young couple home when they were fit to be released, and would take care of the farm in the meantime.

'I'll organise for a taxi to take you home—unless you'd like to drive the Citroën and come back for me later?' Guy offered as he drew up in the ambulance bay to make it easier for the emerging staff to offload their charges.

'Can we leave any decisions until we see what the situation is like inside?' Val suggested, strangely loath to leave him—as though that would signal the end of the magical interlude between them.

'OK. I'll just go and park this out of the way, then I'll see you inside.'

Jacqui was the first person Val saw when she made her way through to the changing-room.

'*Qu-est-ce qui s'est passé?*' she demanded, seeing Val's bedraggled clothing.

'*Un arbre, une inondation, un feu, une jambe casseé et un enfant,*' she enumerated, amazed, as she ran through the list, at exactly how much had happened since she'd left the hospital yesterday.

At least the questions Jacqui threw at her while she changed into her borrowed uniform and smartened herself up a bit stopped her from thinking about the other events that had happened after midnight. *They* were strictly between Guy and herself.

The department was kept fairly busy with a spate of minor injuries, most of them caused when people were desperately trying to rescue their belongings or their livestock.

Suddenly the flu epidemic seemed to be a long way in the past as they concentrated on burns and cuts and broken limbs.

Most would heal with the minimum of attention, but there were always the occasional ones which made even Val wince.

One elderly farmer's wife nearly reduced her to tears as she hobbled into the department on a home-made splint.

For the first time Val's French completely deserted her and she left it to Jacqui to translate as she lifted up the hem of the traditional black skirt and untied the contraption she found when they finally managed to get her up on to the bed.

It transpired that the old lady had slipped and fallen when she was trying to drive their precious cows to higher ground and had hurt her leg.

Instead of abandoning them to their fate, the indomi-table little lady had found two lengths of wood and had bound them to her leg with strips torn from her petticoat so that she wouldn't have to put any weight on the leg that hurt.

Val examined the makeshift contraption and found that the wood had been carefully positioned so that she had been using the splint almost as a short stilt, the weight of her body being borne by the bindings holding the other ends of the wood to her thigh.

'*Il faut faire une radio, je crois,*' Val commented with a wince when she saw the swelling and discoloration at intervals along the leg. Just the angle at which she was holding her foot made it certain that there was at least one break.

Even though she was white and shaken the little woman left them all laughing when she finally set off on her journey to the X-ray department with her glee that just as she'd managed to see her own cows settled safely, they were joined by a neighbour's bull which must have escaped somehow.

'Nine months' time, I should have at least one good strong calf without having to pay him for the services of his bull!' she chortled with glee.

Medically speaking, the woebegone group of English tourists who turned up next were almost light relief after Madame Vigne's traumatic injury, although their miserable night of sickness and diarrhoea had left them all without a sense of humour.

Their relief at finding an English nurse was quite comical as, this being their first trip to France and not understanding the language, they had dreaded having to mime their complaints to a foreigner.

'It's all very well going into a shop and saying

''Moo'' if you want some milk,' one of them muttered, 'but I draw the line at a graphic demonstration of Montezuma's Revenge.'

Staffing levels were nearly back to normal, with most of the flu sufferers back on their feet, and it was when Jacqui caught Val yawning for the third time that she suggested that a quick word with the senior nursing officer would release her from her temporary staff status so that she could catch up on some sleep.

Val glanced at her watch as she strapped it back on her wrist. She grimaced at the state of the clothes she'd had to put back on to travel home but nothing could dampen the excitement which was slowly building inside her.

Seven-thirty, she gloated, hugging the fact to herself as she calculated how many hours it was until Guy would be taking her out for the promised dinner.

She'd wondered if the events of the last twenty-four hours would have made a difference to the arrangements, but he'd made a point of confirming them, meeting her outside the door when she'd gone to make her farewells to the staff she'd been working with.

'Seven-thirty?' he'd queried cryptically, his face no less handsome in her eyes in spite of the fact his beard was still ragged from the burn.

'Yes, please,' she'd replied politely, in spite of the excitement bubbling up inside her—then panicked. 'What should I wear?' she demanded. 'I haven't brought anything really dressy. . .'

'Wear something you feel comfortable in, and we'll choose somewhere to suit it,' he suggested, and pushed the door open for her.

Val was pleasantly surprised by how many of her new colleagues had managed to put in an appearance.

'Come back to visit us another time,' she was invited.

'But leave your English weather behind before you come,' added another voice, and there was general laughter.

'It would be no trouble to find a job for you,' volunteered one of the administrators. 'With all the new regulations in Europe, someone with your qualifications and experience would be welcome.'

Val blinked. She hadn't even thought about the possibility of moving to France, but once the seed had been planted the idea began to grow.

Logically there was no reason why she couldn't pursue her career in France—she'd certainly proved that her study of the language had helped her to cope with most situations in the last few days, and there was no reason why she shouldn't intensify her efforts and learn the more specialised vocabulary she would need if she was to work full time in France. . .

The taxi Guy had arranged for her was already pulling up outside his house when she hauled in the reins on her galloping daydreams.

If she was honest with herself the central figure of the imagined scenario was Guy, and until they'd had a chance to talk about what had happened last night and whether there was any future for them together there was no point in planning any career changes. Her energy would be better spent concentrating on getting ready for their meal tonight.

CHAPTER NINE

'*BONSOIR, Valentine. Quelle belle robe!*' exclaimed her beaming hostess when Val finally made her way down to the salon that evening.

'*Merci beaucoup.*' Val smiled her pleasure at the compliment, delighted to be able to return it wholeheartedly. Simone de Bourges was looking wonderful— a far cry from the confused, pain-racked individual Val had first met.

As she walked across to sit on the end of a nearby settee, Val caught a quick glimpse of herself in the ornate mirror hanging over the fireplace, surrounded by the quiet elegance of Guy's family home.

It helped her confidence as she waited for him to appear that she not only felt good but looked good, too.

She'd indulged in a sinfully long bath with just a sprinkle of her favourite perfume in place of bath oil and had washed and conditioned her hair to within an inch of its life, determined that at least once Guy would see her with perfectly clean, shiny hair.

Her choice of clothing had been easy as she'd only brought one smart dress with her. She certainly hadn't been expecting to meet anyone as devastating as Guy or she might have been tempted to buy something extravagant.

At least her final check in the mirror had confirmed that the fluid lines of the fine, silky jersey dress fitted her even better than she remembered—all the exercise over the last few days must have continued the hard work she'd been putting in on getting herself fit.

The rich jewel tone of the burgundy fabric complemented the heightened colour in her cheeks and her eyes were gleaming softly with anticipation as she slid her feet into slender shoes.

She knew that the weather wasn't warm enough to go out without another layer but couldn't face wearing her faithful coat again. This time the hip-length jacket from her trouser suit would have to do duty, and she folded it neatly over one arm as she let herself out of her bedroom.

She'd heard Guy arrive about fifteen minutes earlier and guessed he'd been held up at the hospital, but that was part and parcel of a doctor's life and she would just have to accept it if he was going to ask her to. . .

She drew in a sharp breath and stopped those thoughts in their tracks. Guy hadn't even hinted that he was thinking along those lines, so if she didn't want to end up broken-hearted she'd better not get ahead of herself.

'You haven't had much chance to look around Rennes, have you?' Guy's grandmother commented, dragging Val's attention back to her companion.

'Not much,' she agreed. 'But there's still time.'

'What did you want to see? Was there anything in particular?' Her bright eyes flicked up briefly from the tapestry nearing completion.

'Well, I was doing some research into some of the Huguenot families who fled to England. I've been trying to find out if there are any descendants of those same families still in France, because they would be very distantly related.'

Madame de Bourges's attention was caught, especially when Val told her about the results of her enquiries which had led her to Rennes to check for further details.

'And what were the names you have been trying to find? I know that some of the *émigrés* altered their names to fit in more easily in their new country. Are the ones you are looking for much changed from the original French?' Her tapestry lay neglected on her lap as she questioned Val eagerly. 'As you may be able to tell, I, too, have done some research into *our* family connections. Perhaps I will be able to help you.'

'Well, apparently there is some connection with a family name that sounds like de Goussec or de Goussey.' She pulled a wry face as she watched Guy's grandmother frown slightly, then shake her head. It would have been too easy for her to have known just the contact Val needed to complete her search.

'Those two names were just offshoots of my main research, though,' she continued. 'I was hoping that they might help me to pinpoint the correct line of descent if I ended up with more than one possibility.'

'And what name is it that you are most interested in?' Madame's head was tilted slightly to one side, rather like an inquisitive bird, her eyes keenly intent in a way that clearly proclaimed her relationship with Guy.

'My own name—or rather my husband's: Burgess.'

For a moment the elderly woman looked genuinely surprised, then laughed merrily. 'I can't believe it!' she spluttered. 'Have I really known you for all these days and not said anything. . .?'

'Said anything. . .about what?' Val was genuinely puzzled.

'Why, the fact that *your* name is one of the English forms of *my* name!' She lifted the tapestry frame off her lap and propped it on the floor beside her chair, then beckoned Val towards her.

'Do you see the books on that shelf?' She pointed to a collection nearby. 'They are photograph albums and information about the de Bourges family, as far as I have been able to trace them.'

Val was speechless. . .utterly amazed by the turn the conversation had taken. Who would have thought that her hostess might have the very information she had been searching for? She might even be able to point her in the right direction so that she could finally complete her quest.

Then, at last, maybe she would feel that she could finally lay Michael's ghost to rest and get on with her life. . .

'That's the best one,' the eager voice directed her reaching hand. 'That contains the photos of the most recent generations, and I have put in some of the genealogy to say how they are related. . . Do you have any photographs with you? Any lists or family trees?'

'Up in my room,' Val volunteered, her tongue finally working again. 'I brought all my information with me in case I needed to check any of the facts I've already gathered.'

Her hands were trembling with excitement as she laid the album on Simone de Bourges's lap and she had a swift mental image of the three photographs she had in her precious file. If she saw those same features reproduced on one of these pages. . .

'I see Grand-mère has got you looking at all the old photographs.' Guy's husky voice reached her from somewhere behind her, his warm tones pouring over her tense nerves like a soothing balm. 'Have you changed your mind about coming out for a meal? Would you rather see my baby pictures?'

Val had been crouching beside the chair so that her shadow wouldn't obscure the photos but, at the sound of his voice, she straightened up and turned to see him standing in the shadows of the doorway, his athletic figure shown off to perfection in a dark suit as he leaned one shoulder against the wall.

How long had he been there? Had he been listening to their conversation while he watched her, his dark eyes caressing every inch? Had he been remembering the way they had explored each other's bodies in the darkness, their hands taking the place of their eyes as they. . .?

'Guy! You have shaved off your beard!' his grandmother exclaimed in delight, and beckoned him into the brighter light of the room. 'Come and show me what you have been hiding for the last couple of years!'

Val watched with a smile as he took a step forward, waiting to hear how he would respond to his grandmother's teasing.

As he drew closer the light fell across his lean, elegant body and her eyes travelled upwards, visualising the powerful legs as she had seen them in the candlelight last night, the breadth of his chest and the width of his shoulders. . .

Val froze, movement impossible as she focused on his clean-shaven face for the first time.

She barely noticed the gleaming darkness of his hair or the increased colour along his cheek-bones; her eyes were riveted to his terrifying familiarity.

'That bad?' he joked in a husky voice. 'You're not going to run away screaming, are you?'

'Guy! Don't tease the girl,' his grandmother admonished. 'It must be a shock for her to see you without your beard for the first time. . . Although I've never known why you had to grow it in the first place. You're a good-looking man, like your father and grandfather were. . .'

'Perhaps I needed it to preserve an air of mystery,' he said, but Val detected the embarrassment he was hiding under the humour. 'Or I might have been using it to hide from all these women who want to chase me,' he suggested, and grinned at his relative's deprecating expression.

Val's breath caught again as she saw the tell-tale evidence of further similarities—the pair of dimples in his cheeks, very much like Michael's.

'Well, then, Val. You've been very quiet. Have you changed your mind about going out with me?'

'N-no,' she stammered uncertainly as he turned his intent gaze on her, and she managed to dredge up a smile. She desperately needed time to think, but there was no way that she could put him off without involving herself in long explanations to the two of them that she just wasn't ready for yet.

'You promised me a meal and you're not getting out of it that easily. . .'

Her attempt at a chuckle must have been more realistic than she'd thought as Madame de Bourges smiled and waved them on their way, her own friends being due to join her in just a few minutes.

'Have a lovely meal,' she carolled as the two of them paused while Guy took her jacket from the arm of the settee and held it out for her. 'And a happy Valentine's Day!'

Val stiffened with horror, one arm suspended halfway into the sleeve of her jacket.

It was Valentine's Day?

How could she have forgotten. . .?

'Val?'

The tone of Guy's voice told her that it wasn't the first time he'd said her name.

'I'm sorry, Guy. What did you say?' It took an effort but she managed to drag herself together into some semblance of normality.

'I asked what was wrong,' he said, a frown drawing his dark brows together. 'Are you sure you're feeling all right? We don't have to go out tonight if you'd rather not.'

What was the alternative? Val thought bleakly. Staying in and remembering how terrible last year had been, with its endless self-recrimination and endless replaying of memories. . .

'No! No, I. . .I just realised that I'd forgotten. . .forgotten what day it was,' she said lamely.

'Was it important?' he prompted as he smoothed his hands soothingly over her shoulders.

'No. . . Well. . .' She grimaced and looked up at him, startled all over again by his resemblance to Michael. 'Just that it's my birthday,' she volunteered with an apologetic shrug.

'*Ah! Bon anniversaire!*' Madame was obviously delighted to learn of the occasion. '*Et c'est l'année bissextile!*'

Val's forehead pleated as she tried to understand the new phrase.

'Leap year,' Guy translated and laughed, wagging a warning finger at his grandmother. 'But not leap-year day—that's another fortnight away!'

It was obvious from his reaction that there was some special significance and Val would have loved to have asked Madame de Bourges whether the French had the same customs about leap year as she did, but she didn't have the courage—not in front of Guy.

As he settled her in the front seat of the Citroën she had to admit that the impetuous thought which had suddenly leapt into her head after the by-play between Guy and his grandmother had certainly kept her mind off the anger and sadness she'd been expecting.

As she watched him rounding the front to join her in the intimate confines of the car, she nearly chuckled as she tried to imagine Guy's reaction if she took advantage of the custom she'd been told—that on leap-year day, instead of waiting for a proposal, a woman could propose to the man of her choice. . .and if he turned her down he had to buy her a silk dress or a pair of kid gloves!

They didn't talk much on the way to the restaurant Guy had chosen, each of them seeming to be preoccupied with their own thoughts.

The flurry of activity as they arrived at the restaurant and were shown to their table prevented Val from doing much more than glance at Guy, amazed that in the middle of all the turmoil going on in her mind she noticed that the tie he was wearing exactly matched the colour of her dress.

'I didn't have a chance to tell you before but you look beautiful,' he murmured, his husky voice lowered so that it reached only her ears.

'I think what you mean is you're pleased to find out what I look like when I'm not soaking wet,' she retorted lightly, trying to combat the quiver of pleasure she felt at the compliment.

She'd been almost relieved when they were shown into seats which were positioned side by side, glad that she wouldn't be spending the evening facing him. . . seeing the face which, now that he'd shaved his beard off, should have been that of a stranger but was actually more familiar than ever.

Now she wasn't so certain it was a good idea to sit beside him. If she'd found it too disturbing to look at him she could always have concentrated on her meal. This way was so much more intimate. Every time either of them moved their bodies brushed, shoulders and elbows and thighs, and she was jolted by a sharp current of awareness.

When their waiter returned with the water Val had requested, she reached for it eagerly to relieve her dry throat and determined to pull herself together.

At this rate Guy was going to wonder what was the matter with her and she wasn't ready to answer questions—she had too many of her own she wanted answered.

An hour ago she had been daydreaming about the possibility of moving to France. If she was right about the attraction that was growing between Guy and herself, it could have provided the basis for a relationship—even marriage.

Now she didn't know what to think.

Was she really falling in love with him?

He was a wonderful man, kind, clever, funny, passionate and a superb doctor. . .everything she could ever need.

But in the back of her mind there was a terrible suspicion—had her subconscious had a hand in the growing attraction? Had she recognised that under the cover of his beard was the man who could be mistaken for her husband's twin?

'You're very quiet,' Guy commented when the waiter departed and Val realised that she must have already finished her first course because her entrée was waiting in front of her.

'I'm sorry,' she murmured, stung by remorse that Guy had made the effort to take her out and she'd hardly said a word to him so far.

'You looked as if you were lost in memories,' he prompted gently. 'From your expression they weren't all happy ones—is that because you're away from home on your birthday?'

'No!' Val shook her head emphatically. 'That's not the problem.'

'So there *is* a problem,' he said astutely, and Val resigned herself to the inevitable.

'Everything always happens on Valentine's Day,' she admitted with a sigh. 'My birthday, the day I met Michael, the day I got married. . .' she paused to swallow '. . .the day I was widowed and lost my little boy. . .'

Her voice died and she found herself staring at the food on her plate, her cutlery clenched in white-knuckled hands.

'I'm sorry.' One warm hand covered one of hers and squeezed gently. 'So many good things, so many happy memories—all spoilt by one bad one.'

He took his hand away again and she felt bereft, her fingers cold in spite of the warm room.

'Val,' he said quietly, 'you didn't have to force yourself to come out. If you'd told me about it, I'd have understood.'

'Oh, Guy. It's not like that,' she said earnestly, the sadness of his voice snapping her out of her preoccupation and forcing her to make the effort to explain.

'Until your grandmother wished us a happy Valentine's Day I had completely forgotten what day it was.' She looked up into his eyes and her heart clenched when she saw the shadows there. 'I was really looking forward to coming out tonight—I even washed my hair!'

The silly comment drew a rusty chuckle out of him and she saw the tension in his shoulders relax.

'Anyway,' she added, lowering her voice to a husky whisper, 'if you think about it, it's been Valentine's Day since just after midnight last night and I can remember being spectacularly happy right from the beginning. . .'

She saw the pupils of his eyes dilate as the meaning of her words struck him, and his mouth began to curve up into the wicked grin that turned her stomach inside out.

'Yes,' he said hoarsely, and when she saw his eyes focus on her mouth she couldn't help but touch her tongue-tip to her lower lip, as though she could still taste his kisses there. . .'Spectacular is a good word for it. . .' he murmured intimately, and fixed her gaze with his.

'*Monsieur?*'

The worried voice at his elbow drew Guy's eyes away from hers and he had to spend several minutes persuading the *maître d'* that there was nothing wrong with their meals—in fact, they were wonderful and the two of them were enjoying the food enormously.

'I think you overdid that a bit,' Val muttered out of the side of her mouth, dying to laugh aloud.

'Dammit, woman, what do you expect me to say?' he grumbled in return. 'Should I tell him, I'm sorry, young man, but I can't remember what I'm eating because the woman sitting beside me is seducing me with words and the shape of her mouth and the feel of her thigh against mine. . .?'

'Guy!' she exclaimed breathlessly, all interest in the meal disappearing at the import of his words, her eyes gazing helplessly into his.

'Dammit! Let's get out of here,' he said urgently, crumpling his table napkin in one hand.

'What. . .? Why?' Val blinked, startled when his hand found hers under the edge of the table and he threaded his fingers through hers to urge her to her feet. 'Where would we go?'

'Anywhere,' he breathed vehemently as he glanced up at the *maître d'* bearing down on them in agitation.

Val was certain that it would take a long time for Guy to extricate himself from the embarrassing situation but within minutes she was scampering along beside him, trying to keep up with his much longer strides as they hurried towards his car.

She was certain that she must be wearing a big soppy smile—she hadn't felt this light-hearted in years.

'Where are we going?' she repeated, still breathless with laughter from his performance as 'doctor on call receiving message to perform life-saving deeds' as she leant against the side of the vehicle while he unlocked her door.

'Home,' he replied succinctly.

'But we can't—your mother's entertaining friends. They'll all want to know why we're back so early.'

'They won't know,' he said smugly, the killer grin flashing at her under the streetlight. 'I have my own entrance at the other end of the house so I don't disturb Grand-mère when I come in late from the hospital. We can go in that way without anyone knowing we're back.'

'Convenient,' Val commented acutely, sharp knives

ripping through her at the thought of all the women who must have been taken in through his private entrance.

'Put your claws away, cat,' he scolded knowingly, obviously deducing her thoughts from her tone of voice. 'It hasn't got a revolving door—in fact, you're the first female, apart from my grandmother, who's been to my apartment.'

Val heard the sincerity in his voice and, in spite of the fact that she hardly knew him, her heart swelled in her chest as she recognised his intrinsic honesty.

As he turned the car into the drive Guy dipped the headlights and allowed the car to coast past the front of the house, bringing it to a halt in the shadows around the back.

'Real cloak-and-dagger stuff,' Val giggled softly, her high spirits restored as she closed the door with a quiet click and followed in his footsteps to the side door, their path lit by a security light showing through the transom window above the door.

He dropped the catch on the lock and turned to face her, his back against the heavy wooden door.

'Come here,' he growled, holding both arms out to her and she flew towards him as eagerly as a homing pigeon at the end of a long journey.

'Oh, Guy,' she breathed as she wound her arms around his waist and lay her head on his shoulder with a sigh.

For long seconds they stood there as she revelled in his warmth and strength, breathing in the special blend of soap and musk which she would recognise anywhere as unique to Guy's skin.

'Val,' he murmured as he cradled her head against him with one broad palm, and she could hear the steady rhythm of his heartbeat as clearly as if he was naked.

Impatience surged through her, shocking her with its unaccustomed heat as she remembered how virile he had looked in the few seconds she had seen him by candlelight.

Tonight they would have the chance to explore each other with their eyes, as well as their hands and lips.

'Are you going to give me a guided tour?' she prompted huskily, looking up at the dark blaze of his eyes. She knew instinctively that he was longing for their first kiss as much as she was, but if he brought his mouth down those few inches to meet hers they might never leave the spartan coolness of this little hallway.

'Only if you want one,' he replied gruffly as he loosened his arms and captured one of her hands, intertwining their fingers as he led her towards the narrow, twisting staircase. 'I can think of several things I'd rather do than show you round my accommodation. . .'

'Perhaps I should get you to tell me about the other things you'd rather be doing,' she said provocatively, and was amazed to realise that the sexy chuckle which echoed around the ivory walls had come from her.

What was happening to her? Why was she so different? Was it because she had finally fallen in love with the one man who was the perfect match for her?

As she followed him up the stairs her thoughts were suddenly crystal-clear.

She had loved Michael and had willingly married him and carried his son but, as she looked back, she could see that there had been no true partnership between them—no meeting of minds and souls.

She hadn't missed it because she hadn't realised that such a thing could exist—until she met Guy. . .

She stifled a wry laugh when she remembered her

fears that she had only been attracted to Guy because her subconscious had recognised his resemblance to Michael. If anything, it was the reverse. She was attracted to him *in spite of* the resemblance, the person behind the face drawing her far more than she had ever believed possible.

At the top of the stairs Guy drew her out of her introspection and back into his arms with a husky groan.

'Ah, Val, with that expression on your face you're irresistible.' He tightened his arms around her and she could feel the fine tremor in his muscles as he fought for control. 'May I ask a favour?' he murmured against the soft skin of her throat.

'Anything,' she agreed simply, knowing beyond a doubt that this was the way things were meant to be between them.

'Ever since you had your nightmare I've been fantasising about you sitting up in that bed surrounded by all those pillows and it's been driving me mad. . .' He paused as though trying to decide whether to continue, but Val tilted her head back to look at him.

'Most women would choose the four-poster but. . . me too,' she admitted huskily, remembering her reaction to the stunned expression on his face when she'd sat there with the covers around her waist. . .'Only I've been imagining you in it. . .with me!'

His deep groan seemed to be dragged up from the depths.

'Then what do you say to the two of us satisfying our imaginations?' he suggested and drew her towards the doorway which linked his domain with the corridor leading to Val's room.

The noise on the polished wood on either side of the beautiful carpet runner sounded very loud when Val's heels tapped in the subdued light, and she held Guy's hand for balance while she slipped them off and clutched them in her free hand.

Their feet began moving faster and faster the nearer they came to her door and it was difficult to remember to keep their voices down when they were chuckling and scampering on tiptoe like two children bent on mischief.

As soon as they reached her room and were closing the door behind them, the mood changed.

Suddenly they were enclosed in a private sanctuary, the soft peachy light of the bedside lamp reminiscent of the glow of the candle beside the four-poster bed just twenty-four hours ago as they gazed compulsively at each other.

Val's heart was beating so fast that her breasts were shuddering, her breathing growing shallow as she anticipated the pleasures to come.

'I'm afraid to touch you,' he whispered, his hands hanging almost awkwardly at his sides as he looked at her. 'I've been dreaming of this for so long that I'm afraid if I reach out you'll disappear.'

'I won't disappear,' she promised, bending to place her shoes on the floor before she took the final step into his arms. 'I'm not going anywhere. . .'

CHAPTER TEN

VAL unlocked her door and dragged herself inside. Her luggage felt like a load of bricks and her head was throbbing as if it was going to explode.

After twelve hours of travelling, much of it spent huddling out of sight to avoid the pity her tears would elicit, she was shattered.

'I'm not going anywhere. . .' she'd said, the words a vow straight from her overflowing heart, and yet here she was on the other side of the English Channel, back in her own flat.

She would have thought she had no more tears to shed but, at the thought of the heartbreaking events of the last few hours, they welled up in her eyes again. Was there no end to them? Apparently not, when her heart still felt as if it had been ripped out by the roots.

The shrill sound of the phone sliced through her anguish and she stood frozen with indecision while her machine cut in to answer.

Convulsively she raised one hand towards the receiver as if she could will the voice on the other end to be the one she wanted to hear, but whoever it was rang off without leaving a message.

The little light glared balefully at her to tell her that other people had rung too, but she couldn't dredge up the energy to listen to the messages. All she wanted to do was to stand under the shower until she emptied the tank and then fall into bed to sleep the clock round. Perhaps oblivion would help her to cope with her misery. Perhaps when she woke up the world would look a better place.

Five minutes later she was huddled in a sobbing heap under the bedclothes.

Would nothing go right?

Just the act of undressing, ready to step into the shower cubicle, had reminded her of the way Guy had helped her out of her clothes when her hands had been too sore; his insistence on massaging the pain out of her shoulders. She had despaired that she would never be able to take a shower again without thinking about it. . . then the icy cold water had landed in the middle of her back and she had leapt out, shrieking with shock.

How could she have forgotten that she'd switched off the immersion heater before she went away to save money? Of course there was no hot water. . .

Her bedraggled figure had stared back at her from the mirror, her hair once more hanging around her face in horribly familiar rats-tails, and she had wailed aloud, grabbing a towel and racing through to the bedroom.

What chance did she have of forgetting Guy when everything seemed to remind her of him? Even her wet hair, for heaven's sake. . .

She curled up tighter, her arms wrapped around herself in search of comfort as she finally gave in to the awful memories.

It hadn't started out that way.

Guy had held her so tenderly—as if she were a rare and precious blossom—and when her heart had overflowed and she'd whispered her love to him, he'd repeated the words too, promising that they'd be together for ever. . .

For ever?

Her mouth twisted bitterly.

He must have a different definition of for ever to hers. . .

As far as she was concerned, for ever meant love and trust; for ever meant caring and sharing with the one who was the other half of your soul; for ever meant not jumping to conclusions and refusing to listen to an explanation, even when things might look bad. . .

The scene replayed itself in slow motion through her mind like some dreadful video film and she was filled with the frantic desire to be able to press the stop button, knowing what was going to happen but powerless to change it.

It had been the ultimate fantasy—the one she'd hardly dared to visualise. . .

She'd been so happy, his words of love echoing in her ears and imprinted on her lips as he'd slowly removed her silky dress, his whispered words of praise mingling with her own as she opened the buttons of his shirt with trembling fingers.

As if he couldn't bear to be apart from her, he'd lifted her in his arms and carried her over to the bed, laying her tenderly on the smooth white sheets and then straightening up to look at her, his darkly gleaming eyes as potent a caress as any touch.

Strangely, she hadn't felt a trace of embarrassment, her skin warmed by the heat of his gaze as his expression told her how much he desired her.

'Come in to bed with me,' she whispered, holding her arms out to him yearningly. 'I need to hold you.'

He began to lean forward, then paused briefly to reach for his wallet with a grimace.

'We forgot this at the farm,' he murmured as he stretched his powerful length beside her. 'And while I'd like nothing better than to watch you carrying our baby, I'm hoping I can have you to myself for a while. . .'

She smiled, her lips quivering softly at the mental image of her own body cradling his child, then held her hand out for the small package he'd retrieved, showing her acceptance of his reason for delaying that pleasure.

His eyes widened, his pupils dilating at the significance of her outstretched hand, too engrossed in watching her to concentrate on placing his wallet on the bedside cabinet.

There was a sharp slap as he dislodged something and tipped it onto the polished floor.

'Sorry,' he whispered, glancing distractedly towards the sound to see what had fallen before he turned back to face her, his eyes intent on her hands as she tore the packet open.

Suddenly he jerked upright and turned away from her to gaze down at the floor beside the bed.

'What the. . .?' He bit the expletive off as he swung his long legs over the side of the bed and sat up. 'What is this?' he demanded ominously.

Val slid across towards him and leaned over the edge of the bed. She rested her hand on his shoulder to steady herself and was startled when he flinched away from her, his eyes riveted on the floor.

The sound they'd heard was her precious folder falling, and she could see that the impact had caused several of the contents to slide partway out. Her own neat writing was much in evidence, as was the edge of a chart of the Burgess family tree that she'd been trying to compile.

As far as she could see nothing had been damaged, and for a moment she couldn't understand Guy's reaction. He'd known that she was researching into the

Huguenot connections of the Burgess family—had even kept her company at the *Museé de Bretagne* while she looked for more clues as to the connections with the de·Goussey/de Goussec families.

'Oh, God. . .' she whispered when she saw the photograph that had slid just that little bit further, coming to rest against the edge of the carpet.

If it had to be one of the photographs lying there, why couldn't it have been Simon's or. . .? But it was Michael's—his graduation photo with his eyes full of life and laughter. The one that made him look so much like. . .

'Where did you get that photo?' There was a chill in his voice that she had never heard before and it tied her tongue in knots as she watched him reach forward, the muscles in his shoulder and arm stretching under the oiled silk of his skin as he picked up the tell-tale oblong.

'Guy. . .I can explain. . .' she began, knowing in her heart that she couldn't have chosen a worse time, but he wasn't listening—his eyes were riveted on the photo.

'This isn't my. . . Who *is* this?' He whirled to face her, holding the picture towards her, his eyes glacial.

'M-Michael,' she whispered as her heart sank like a stone. 'That's. . . That was my husband, Michael Burgess.'

There were several seconds of silence which felt as if they lasted a thousand years as he looked down at the likeness he held.

'So *this* is the reason you were so amenable to keeping an old lady company. . .' he said harshly, the expression of utter disdain on his face freezing the breath in her throat so that she was unable to utter a word.

'I know you told me some sob-story about being all alone and looking for long-lost family. . . You must have thought you'd hit the jackpot when you realised you'd got a chance to replace the man you lost with an identical model.'

'No!' The denial was torn from her as she scrambled backwards and dragged the edge of the sheet up to cover her nakedness from his searing gaze. She hadn't even known that Guy resembled Michael until he'd shaved his beard off—until after she'd watched him risk his own life to save that of a complete stranger and realised that she loved him. . . 'No! It's not true! You're not. . .'

'What? Not identical?' He brandished the photo at her like an aggressive attorney waving evidence under the nose of a less than truthful witness. 'Identical enough for your purposes, obviously—otherwise why would you have fallen into my arms after just a few days when there's been no one in your life since *he* died?

'And I nearly fell for it!' he added, his voice an unflattering mixture of self-condemnation and admiration. 'I thought there was a genuine rapport between us. You truly had me believing the attraction was real. . . My God! I was actually going to *propose* to you!'

'Oh, Guy!' Her heart was breaking at the pain he was unable to conceal, knowing it was so unnecessary. . . 'It wasn't like that. It *wasn't* because you look like Michael. . .'

'Then why didn't you tell me?' he demanded, his very tone an accusation. 'Why didn't you tell me it was *my* family you were looking into? Why didn't you show me the photo?' He flicked it across the bed towards her as if he couldn't bear to touch it any more, and bent to gather up the clothes he'd discarded so haphazardly. . . so eagerly.

'Because I didn't *know* about the connection with your family,' she said frantically as she saw her chance for happiness slipping through her fingers, desperately trying to find the words which would convince him that she was telling the truth. 'Because it didn't *matter* that you looked like—'

'Didn't know!' he scoffed. 'I might have swallowed that if I didn't know how much research Grand-mère has done. She would have told you if you'd mentioned it openly.'

He'd thrust his feet into his trousers one at a time, magnificently unconcerned that she was looking on his nakedness with despair and futile longing.

'Please, Guy,' she called, desperate for one last chance to explain as he strode towards the door with the rest of his clothes in a bundle under his arm. She'd risen to her knees, one hand reaching out in supplication as the rumpled sheet fell away from her.

'Very tempting!' he rasped as his eyes roved insultingly over the exposed curves. 'But not quite enough to persuade a wedding ring out of me!' And he let himself out of the room.

The hurt had been too deep, too sudden, for tears, so she'd been utterly dry-eyed when she'd hastily packed her belongings in her bags and dressed herself in warm clothes for travelling.

A last-minute nudge from her conscience made her write a brief note of apology to her hostess, then she was standing by the gateway waiting for her taxi to arrive—not even wanting the vehicle to trespass on the driveway in her effort to leave as swiftly as possible.

At Rennes station she'd been lucky enough to board a train immediately and had spent the entire journey with her face turned blankly towards the window as tears streamed silently down her face.

When she couldn't have cared what happened to her, she made all her connections for her return to England with the smoothness of a journey planned for months, only managing to stop the flow of tears long enough to pay her fare and find a corner seat before she was overwhelmed by misery again.

And here she was, a sodden heap under the covers of her own bed, still unable to understand how the happiest day of her life had turned into such a disaster.

She dozed fitfully, tossing and turning as she replayed the scene in her head until she sat up in disgust.

'Enough!' she declared aloud and reached for her saggy old towelling bathrobe, tying it tightly around her waist before she set off for the kitchen. 'I need to get my head straight and I need to eat, and no damned suspicious, distrustful man is going to stop me!'

The sound of the determined words in the silent space of her flat stiffened her shoulders and raised her chin as she went in search of the sliced loaf hidden in her freezer.

'Soup and toast,' she decreed, her hands moving swiftly to open the tin while the bread thawed and browned. '*Then* I'll decide what I'm going to do. . .'

The light on the answering machine beckoned her as she set the tray down on the table beside it, and she gave in to the temptation.

Beep. . .! 'Lily here,' intoned Staff Nurse Balewa's voice. 'If you hear this before Saturday morning and feel like joining the fray. . .help! They're going down like flies with this wretched flu. Hope to see you!'

Beep. . .! 'You couldn't make that Friday, could you?'

Val couldn't help chuckling at the sound of desperation in the second message.

Beep. . .! There were several seconds of silence filled only with the sound of crackling on the line before the connection was broken, and Val just had time to wonder if Lily had decided against leaving another plea before the fourth message began.

Beep. . .! 'Val. . .?' The sound of the husky voice was unmistakable and sent an electric shock right through her body. 'Are you home. . .? Are you safe. . .?' He paused and she was almost certain that she could hear the sound of his breathing before he cut the connection.

The machine whirred while it rewound the tape and set the message tally back to nought, then subsided into silence.

Val had been about to take the first bite from her toast as Guy's voice had filled her little room, and her hand was still suspended in mid-air in front of her mouth when the final click came.

'Damn him!' she muttered through clenched teeth as she deposited the toast back on the plate with a trembling hand. 'What's he playing at?' She scrambled up out of the chair and strode backwards and forwards across the limited area in front of the gas fire. 'As if he cares whether I'm safe!'

The surge of anger that swept through her achieved what all her previous determination hadn't managed and she finally knew that she was going to survive.

'OK, Mr Self-righteous, you've made your point,' she said icily as she sat herself back down in front of her tray of food, a sneaking feeling of guilt assailing her that her abrupt departure would have concerned Madame de Bourges.

'I'm going to have my food and then I'll phone and leave a message so that no one will be worried about me, and then you're history!'

She was as good as her word, putting the tray aside as soon as it was empty and reaching for the phone, determinedly ignoring the tremor in her crossed fingers as she pressed the buttons.

'Allô?'

Val gave a deep sigh of relief as she recognised Berthe's voice and uncrossed her fingers.

'Berthe? C'est Valentine. . .'

'Ah, mademoiselle! Monsieur Guy n'est pas ici. . .'

Val smiled tightly as she heard Berthe's voice telling her that Guy had taken his grandmother for a check-up at the hospital.

She told herself fiercely that she was grateful that there was no chance of hearing his voice, then asked the friendly woman to pass on her good wishes to Madame de Bourges and let her know she'd arrived in England safely.

She felt quite limp when she put the receiver down, as if it had taken all her energy to cut the final connections with her stay in France, but the big dark hole inside her told her that she wouldn't be able to forget that time quite so easily.

'Now all I have to do is find a way to wipe them out of my mind,' she muttered aloud in an attempt at drowning out the warning voice in her head as she carried her tray through to her tiny kitchen and washed up the few items.

'Work!' she announced in the same tone of voice a seaman must have used when he sighted land, knowing that it would be her salvation, and she went back to the phone to contact the hospital. If things were as bad as Lily seemed to think, she would be back in the thick of things before she could draw breath. . .

'Bronchiolitis,' Dick Trask announced as he shouldered his way past the curtain with his little burden just two minutes after Val arrived on duty.

'This is Philip Dennis,' he continued briskly. 'He's eight months old. Apparently just a little ''stuffy'' when he went to bed last night, but when he began fighting for breath they phoned for their GP who called us out. He arrested twice on the way here. . .'

The paramedic lay the distressed little boy down and his colleague deposited the ventilator and monitoring equipment around their little patient.

The consultant fired the usual questions, his staff taking over the IV drip and reconnecting the various tubes and wires to the hospital oxygen system and the monitors while he made his own examination, the handover swift and expert as he took over responsibility for the little lad.

'Parents?' Val prompted, then bent over to draw the blood samples they needed, her voice a soothing murmur in case her little charge could hear her.

'Following us in,' Dick confirmed. 'They had to settle another child with neighbours.'

As he spoke there was the sound of hurried footsteps and worried voices wanting to know where their little boy had been taken.

'All yours,' Dick confirmed wryly. 'See you again.' He signalled to his colleague and they picked up the mobile ambulance equipment and took themselves out of the way.

'Right,' said the consultant, 'let's get him on humidified oxygen and start antibiotic cover while we establish which virus he's picked up. Be prepared to hook up the positive pressure breathing—we might have to administer epinephrine if his breathing doesn't improve. . .'

'Has anyone asked the parents whether there's any family history of asthma?' Val asked as she handed over the marked blood samples for immediate lab analysis.

'Can you do that, Sister, and check how soon they'll be ready for him up in ICU?'

Young Philip's arrival seemed to set the trend for the day. Even with all the available staff working at full stretch, the waiting area rarely appeared to be less than half-full and emergencies were coming in as frequently as ever.

For Val it was almost like an action replay of her time in the hospital in Rennes, with the cancellation of all but emergency operations and the clearing of as many beds as possible to cope with the influx of distressed patients, many of them elderly, who were being struck down by this particularly virulent strain of the virus.

By the time she arrived home she felt as if she'd just worked a double shift straight through, her feet and legs aching and her stomach rattling empty.

'Soup and toast—again!' she groaned when she looked in the fridge and remembered that she'd forgotten to shop on the way home, but really she was too tired to care.

The sight of her cases, still piled against the wall just inside her bedroom, barely drew more than a grimace before she dragged herself into the bathroom.

She was just falling into a deep, exhausted sleep

when she thought she heard the telephone ring, but as the answering machine switched on she was too tired to care.

She didn't sleep well, her dreams peopled with dark, enclosed places and shadowy figures who wouldn't listen when she called out to them.

The fact that she'd totally forgotten to set her alarm didn't help matters the next morning and it was only the ringing of the telephone that dragged her to wakefulness in time to leave for work, even though she'd reached the instrument too late to find out who'd called her.

Her last glimpse of the inside of her sitting-room as she pulled the door shut was the little light on her answering machine winking, and her hazy recall of last night told her that she had at least one message waiting but, much as she would have liked to know who the callers were, they would have to wait until she returned home.

She was halfway through a shift that was made more difficult than ever by staff shortages, due to the rampaging flu, when a particularly dim-witted junior told her that the charge nurse had a message for her—but she couldn't remember what it was.

'If that girl's IQ ever catches up with her bra size she'll be dangerous,' Val muttered when she finally managed to track Tom down. 'Were we ever that gormless?'

'What. . .you and me? Never!' he said staunchly.

'Thank God for small mercies,' she said. 'Now, was there a message or did she get that wrong too?'

'You've been holding out on us, darling,' he accused with a grin and pointed over his shoulder towards the staff rest-room. 'Visitor waiting for you and, as you haven't had your break yet, you might as well take the chance to grab a cup of coffee.'

'Who?' Her feet were already taking her in the direction of a reviving hot drink.

'Off you go and find out!' He waggled his eyebrows up and down insinuatingly and made a shooing motion with one hand.

Val's first thought had been that Guy was waiting for her, and she'd been hard put to keep her face straight as her heart leapt into her throat. Then she remembered his cold anger when he'd left her bedroom and she knew that he was the *last* person she'd find waiting for her.

Well, she thought gratefully, remembering her lack of breakfast this morning, whoever it was, they'd managed to get her a few minutes to sit down with a cup of coffee so she'd be delighted to see them.

When she first pushed the door open she couldn't see anyone waiting and, thinking that her mystery visitor had got tired of waiting and had wandered off for a while, she shrugged and made her way across to the kettle, her stomach rumbling when she caught sight of the open tin of biscuits.

'Hello, Val.'

Her hand clenched in shock when she heard his husky voice behind her, crushing the biscuit she'd just chosen so that fragments exploded across the work surface.

'Guy?' She whirled to face him, her eyes searching him out incredulously as she felt the blood drain from her face and her ears filled with a strange buzzing noise.

'Val!' He shouldered himself away from the wall beside the window and covered the ground between them with a predator's speed, his hands reaching out to catch her as she swayed uncertainly.

'No. . .!' There was little power in her voice but the emotion in it froze him in his tracks. 'Don't. . .*touch*. . . me!' she managed through gritted teeth as she hung onto consciousness by sheer force of will.

Val stepped back from him, her eyes fixed on his face as though she was facing a dangerous animal as she removed herself from the danger of any contact with him. She found the edge of the work surface behind her and gripped it with both hands, releasing the last remaining biscuit crumbs to patter on the floor.

Her heart clenched when she focused on him and saw how pale and tired he looked, his expression withdrawn. He had changed so much since she'd seen him two days ago. What was the matter? Had his grandmother been taken ill?

'Is. . .is your grandmother. . .well?' she asked carefully, not certain if her voice would obey her.

'As well as can be expected, for an elderly lady with a ferocious temper,' he replied drily.

'I'm sorry.' Val glanced away, her pale cheeks gaining a hectic patch of colour as embarrassment flooded her. 'I—I told Berthe to let her know I'd arrived safely but I know it was unforgivably rude of me to leave like that after she'd been so kind—'

'God, Val. Not you!' He cut her off exasperatedly. 'She's not angry with you!'

'Then. . .?'

'It's *me* she's kicked out of the house. . .'

'What?' Now she was completely bewildered.

'I was told to come and make my apologies to you or she'd never let me back inside her doors again.'

'But there's nothing for you to—'

'Please, Val,' he interrupted quietly in a voice full of pain. 'There's so much I need to tell you. Will you let me apologise properly? Then. . .' He gave a characteristically Gallic shrug.

She felt a pang inside her. She'd thought that she would never see that distinctive movement again and she was powerless to refuse his plea.

'Yes,' she whispered, and made her way on shaky legs towards the nearest chair.

'Tonight?' he prompted, stopping her in her tracks. 'It's not really the sort of conversation we can have here.' His glance went around the sparsely functional room and she was suddenly aware of the sounds floating into the room from the busy department just outside the door.

'I suppose you're right,' she agreed on a sigh, leaning against the back of the chair and gripping the back rail with white-knuckled hands. She knew only too well that they could have company at any moment. 'When?'

'I could take you out for a meal this evening?' he offered.

'No.' She rejected him flatly.

Everything in her rebelled at the idea of recreating even a portion of the disastrous ending to Valentine's Day. 'I can't. . .I'll be too tired.' She settled for a half-truth.

'So, shall I come to your home?' he suggested and she nearly laughed. Her home? It had never really been a home, not like his house was a home—a place of warmth and refuge and comfort beyond what was provided by four stout walls and a good fire.

'All right,' she agreed quietly. 'I'll see you at seven.'

He murmured his agreement, pausing briefly as he went to leave the room. Val could feel his eyes on her and a small voice inside her head was screaming for her to turn and meet his gaze, but she couldn't. She needed time to gather herself together before she could hope to meet him on equal terms.

She managed to make herself a cup of coffee and cradled it between both shaking palms to drink it while she marvelled at Guy's appearance in England. Absent-mindedly, she began to help herself to biscuits, hardly noticing that she was devouring one after another as she tried to guess what Guy would talk about this evening.

Something made her glance down at the watch pinned to the front of her uniform and she gasped in dismay. She'd been in here nearly half an hour! What on earth had got into her to desert her colleagues like that?

As ever, work was her salvation, leaving her no time to concentrate on her own worries when she was dealing with severely dehydrated patients with roaring temperatures who desperately needed attention before they could be transferred to one of the precious beds on one of the wards.

She'd contemplated greeting Guy still dressed in the casual clothes she'd worn to travel home, but pride dictated that she made an effort to look her best in spite of her mixed feelings about his visit.

The ring at her doorbell exactly at seven sent her for a last panicked glance in the mirror to check that the collar of her silk blouse was lying smoothly at the neckline of her navy waistcoat and twitched the matching navy skirt straight.

For once he would be seeing her with her make-up
perfect and not a hair out of place. . .

'Come in,' she murmured as she opened the door.
She didn't have the courage, yet, to meet his eyes, but
was forced to grip the knob tightly when he walked
past her and she breathed in his special mixture of soap
and clean healthy male and her knees lost their will to
hold her up.

'Coffee?' she offered, desperate for an excuse
to disappear for a minute to gather her thoughts
together.

'Yes. . . No, thank you,' he overrode his own acceptance. 'Please, Val. . .' He paused and it was his
uncertainty that finally made her look at him face
to face.

'Please,' he repeated, gesturing with an open hand
for her to take a seat. 'Will you sit down? I need. . .'
He drew in a deep breath, his chest expanding under
the fine tailoring of his dark charcoal suit. 'I need to
put things right. . .for both our sakes.'

Silently Val perched on the edge of the settee,
relaxing slightly when he chose her solitary armchair
although he, too, sat uncomfortably close to the edge,
his elbows braced on his thighs and his fingers knotted
together with tension.

She could almost hear his thoughts whirling around
in his head—or was it her own as she veered from
despair to hope and back again as she waited for him
to speak?

'I apologise,' he said grimly, flicking her the briefest
of glances under sooty lashes. 'I know now that I was
wrong and I hurt you. . .'

Silence fell again as his harsh words died away. It

almost seemed as if he had said all that he was going to but Val waited, knowing there was more.

'I've been engaged twice,' he announced suddenly, and the sharp jealousy which ripped into Val dragged her eyes up from their concentration on her white-knuckled fingers to witness the flush of discomfort along his cheek-bones as he continued.

'The first time we were both very young and she wanted the security of being a doctor's wife without the inconvenience of having me work such unsocial hours. The second. . .' He paused with a sigh and shook his head. 'She was. . . Apparently, she was more interested in the house and its contents than she was in me. . . But, of course, I was far too busy to notice. . .'

'But why. . .?' Val gestured helplessly. She was amazed and touched that such an apparently self-possessed and assured man could have had his confidence so badly dented, but. . .

'I was afraid you only wanted me because I looked like your husband—just an echo of your first love,' he said quietly, then held his hand up to prevent her interruption. 'I was afraid because for the first time in my life I was really in love; afraid because if two women had found my position and my possessions more attractive than I was, what would a third be feeling?' There was dark uncertainty in the eyes that gazed so fiercely into hers.

'But, most of all, I was afraid because once Grandmère finished tearing me up in strips and told me that you really *hadn't* known about the connection between our two family names until just before I came in the room everything suddenly fell into place and I realised that I had destroyed the most precious gift in the world.'

Val's eyes filled with tears as she heard the anguish in his voice and knew that it echoed the pain she'd felt when she'd thought she'd lost him.

'Oh, Guy,' she whispered brokenly as she stood up on quivering legs and took two steps towards him. 'Don't you realise that you couldn't be an echo of anyone or anything? I love you for yourself. . .'

Before she could utter another word he surged up out of his seat and met her in the middle of the room, his arms winding tightly around her as he swung her off her feet.

'Oh, my love, my love,' he said hoarsely before he sought her mouth in a kiss which told her that he loved her as much as she loved him.

'Oh, Guy,' she murmured long moments later when he held her cradled firmly on his lap, her head resting trustingly on his broad shoulder. 'I'm sorry I didn't explain things to you. It's just. . .for the first time I felt as if I had truly found the other half of myself. It was bad enough when Michael and Simon died—I'd lost my husband and my son—but this time. . .' She bit her lip while she tried to find the words. 'This time the love is so much deeper that I would have twice as much to lose—I would lose myself as well. . .'

'Ah, Valentine,' he whispered huskily as he held her tightly. 'I should have had more trust in you—more trust in my own feelings, because, in my heart of hearts, I knew that we were right for each other.'

There was a momentary silence while the echoes of his vow died away in the room before Val remembered something he'd said that dreadful night.

'Guy? Did you mean it when you said you were going to propose—?'

Her words were cut off as he shifted suddenly, nearly tipping her onto the floor as he muttered furiously under his breath and tried to force his hand into his jacket pocket.

'I'm sorry,' he murmured penitently as he wrapped both arms around her again and pulled her closer. 'Perhaps I'll manage to do this better next time but. . . Valentine Burgess, will you accept my ring as a pledge that we will be married as soon as I can get you back to Rennes?'

Val dissolved into laughter and flung her arms around his neck.

'I'm sorry, Guy; that was your last chance to practise your delivery of a proposal because I accept and I've absolutely no intention of giving you the chance to propose to anyone else!'

'And you're happy to leave England? To live and work with me in Rennes until our children are born?'

'Our children. . .?' A momentary shadow dimmed her joy. 'Oh, Guy, I don't know whether. . .if we should. . .'

'Shh, my love. Before you say any more let me tell you that my father was almost sixty when he died and my grandfather was in his seventies.'

'Really?' Hope began to blossom again.

'Really,' he confirmed, and retrieved her hand to hold it reassuringly in his warm clasp. 'And you know as well as I do that if you don't develop Huntington's chorea then you can't pass it on.'

'So that means. . .'

'The the de Bourges branch of the family doesn't carry that gene. . .although I'm perfectly happy to wait to start our family until genetic tests can be done. . .'

'No,' she murmured with utter certainty as she reached up to cradle his cheek in her palm, then she smiled as he captured her hand and she watched him slide the ring onto her finger.

As she caught sight of the delicate arrangement of diamonds surrounding a deep blue sapphire her brimming tears of happiness fractured the brilliant sparkle into a million rainbows which would bind the two of them together for ever.

MILLS & BOON®

Medical Romance™

COMING NEXT MONTH

A MIDWIFE'S CHALLENGE by Frances Crowne

Katy Woods resolved never to get involved with men after her disastrous marriage to a bigamist—until she met Dr Mark Hammond. He was irresistible—until she discovered the truth about his ex-girlfriend, which was a haunting reminder of her past...

FULL RECOVERY by Lilian Darcy

Camberton Hospital

Helen Darnell suspected her husband of twenty years, Nick, to be having an affair with a beautiful doctor. Helen tried to quell her fears believing that Nick was faithful to her. Their marriage was teetering on the edge of destruction and only one thing could save it—the truth.

DOCTOR ACROSS THE LAGOON by Margaret Holt

Lucinda Hallcross-Spriggs' journey to Italy for a medical conference took an unexpected turn when she met the devilishly handsome Dr Pino Ponti. She soon succumbed to his relentless charm, but with his restless heart and uneasy past, she surely had no part to play in his future.

LAKELAND NURSE by Gill Sanderson

Zanne Ripley's application for Medical School was unsuccessful—and all because of Dr Neil Calder. Now she had to work with him at the Mountain Activities Centre, but his charm soon broke down her defences. But Neil had a secret...

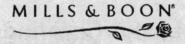

'Happy' Greetings!

Would you like to win a year's supply of Mills & Boon® books? Well you can and they're free! Simply complete the competition below and send it to us by 31st August 1997. The first five correct entries picked after the closing date will each win a year's subscription to the Mills & Boon series of their choice. What could be easier?

ACSPPMTHYHARSI

‗‗‗‗‗ ‗‗‗‗‗‗‗‗‗

TPHEEYPSARA

‗‗‗‗‗ ‗‗‗‗‗‗

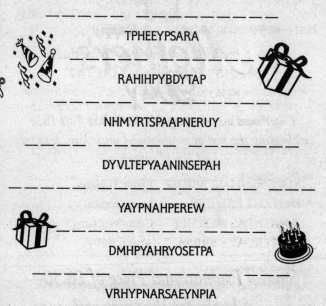

RAHIHPYBDYTAP

‗‗‗‗‗ ‗‗‗‗‗‗‗‗

NHMYRTSPAAPNERUY

‗‗‗‗‗ ‗‗‗‗‗‗ ‗‗‗‗‗‗

DYVLTEPYAANINSEPAH

‗‗‗‗‗ ‗‗‗‗‗‗ ‗‗‗‗‗‗‗

YAYPNAHPEREW

‗‗‗‗‗ ‗‗‗‗‗‗

DMHPYAHRYOSETPA

‗‗‗‗‗ ‗‗‗‗‗‗ ‗‗‗

VRHYPNARSAEYNPIA

‗‗‗‗‗ ‗‗‗‗‗‗‗‗‗

Please turn over for details of how to enter ☞

How to enter...

There are eight jumbled up greetings overleaf, most of which you will probably hear at some point throughout the year. Each of the greetings is a 'happy' one, i.e. the word 'happy' is somewhere within it. All you have to do is identify each greeting and write your answers in the spaces provided. Good luck!

When you have unravelled each greeting don't forget to fill in your name and address in the space provided and tick the Mills & Boon® series you would like to receive if you are a winner. Then simply pop this page into an envelope (you don't even need a stamp) and post it today. Hurry—competition ends 31st August 1997.

Mills & Boon 'Happy' Greetings Competition
FREEPOST, Croydon, Surrey, CR9 3WZ

Please tick the series you would like to receive if you are a winner

Presents™ ❑   Enchanted™ ❑   Medical Romance™ ❑
Historical Romance™ ❑   Temptation® ❑

Are you a Reader Service Subscriber?   Yes ❑   No ❑

Ms/Mrs/Miss/Mr _____

(BLOCK CAPS PLEASE)

Address _____

_____

_____ Postcode _____

(I am over 18 years of age)

One application per household. Competition open to residents of the UK and Ireland only.
You may be mailed with other offers from other reputable companies as a result of this application. If you would prefer not to receive such offers, please tick box. ❑

C7B

mps MAILING PREFERENCE SERVICE

DMA